# BAMBOO KINGDOM

## CREATURES OF THE FLOOD

# BAMBOO KINGDOM

## CREATURES OF THE FLOOD

## ERIN HUNTER

**HARPER**

*An Imprint of HarperCollinsPublishers*

*Special thanks to Rosie Best*

Bamboo Kingdom #1: Creatures of the Flood
Copyright © 2021 by Working Partners Ltd.
Series created by Working Partners Ltd.
Map art © 2021 by Virginia Allyn
Interior art © 2021 by Johanna Tarkela
All rights reserved. Printed in the United States of America.
No part of this book may be used or reproduced in any manner whatsoever without written permission except in the case of brief quotations embodied in critical articles and reviews. For information address HarperCollins Children's Books, a division of HarperCollins Publishers, 195 Broadway, New York, NY 10007.
www.harpercollinschildrens.com

Library of Congress Cataloging-in-Publication Data
Names: Hunter, Erin, author.
Title: Creatures of the flood / Erin Hunter.
Description: First edition. | New York, NY : HarperCollins, [2021] | Series: Bamboo kingdom ; #1 | Audience: Ages 8-12. | Audience: Grades 4-6. | Summary: "Three young pandas set out on separate journeys to save their homes and families in the Bamboo Kingdom"— Provided by publisher.
Identifiers: LCCN 2020045418 | ISBN 978-0-06-302192-1 (hardcover) | ISBN 978-0-06-302193-8 (library binding)
Subjects: CYAC: Pandas—Fiction. | Fantasy.
Classification: LCC PZ7.H916625 Cq 2021 | DDC [Fic]—dc23
LC record available at https://lccn.loc.gov/2020045418

Typography by Corina Lupp
21 22 23 24 25   PC/LSCH   10 9 8 7 6 5 4 3 2 1

First Edition

*For Zhong Jianto, Xu Wei, and Wolffeather,*
*for all your help and for being such kind and welcoming hosts.*
*And for big girls who climb trees.*

*Special thanks to CCPPG for their inspiration and creativity, and for*
*enabling Erin Hunter to bring Bamboo Kingdom to the world.*

# BAMBOO KINGDOM

## CREATURES OF THE FLOOD

# PROLOGUE

ORCHID RISINGTREE REACHED FOR the next paw hold, pulling herself up the slick slope by her claws. The rain soaked into her thick fur, right down to the skin, and she longed to shake herself, but she couldn't. If she lost her grip . . .

"Orchid!" Root growled. "Look out!"

She glanced up just in time. A clump of bamboo, broken loose by the relentless torrent, came crashing down the side of the mountain toward her, its thick stems whipping dangerously around. Orchid roared and threw herself aside. The bamboo seemed to roar back as it sliced through the air close to her ear. She started to slide again, but managed to catch herself on a more firmly rooted tree trunk and look down. As the bamboo tumbled down the mountainside, it passed dangerously close to Root, but he was already altering his path so that it would miss him. She watched as it bounced off the cliff edge, splashed down into the swollen river, and was immediately dragged under by the terrible current.

Orchid paused for a moment, clinging to the tree trunk, catching her breath as her mate climbed toward her, mud and leaves clumped in his black-and-white fur. Sheets of rain battered the back of her head. The whole Bamboo Kingdom seemed to be on the run from the flooding river, the streaming mud where once had been soft moss and comfortable rocks to lie on in the afternoon sun, a scattering of creatures trying to escape the rising waters. She saw a red panda a little way off, its bushy tail thick with mud, panicking as it struggled to climb one of the trees. She longed to help it, but there was nothing she could do.

She had to protect her cubs.

"We can't go much farther," she huffed as Root reached her. "The cubs will be here soon; I can feel it."

"We'll find somewhere safe," Root said. "Look, there's a rock ledge up there. *That* won't be washed away. Just a little farther."

Orchid nodded grimly and turned to press on, pushing with her powerful back legs to reach the next paw hold on the slippery path. She just hoped he was right. Nothing was certain anymore. Perhaps the whole Bamboo Kingdom would be washed away.

But there was nothing to do except keep on climbing, so Orchid climbed, paw by paw, up the ruined mountainside. She kept her gaze fixed on the rock ledge. They were so close, she could imagine the feel of solid ground beneath her. Perhaps there would be shelter, just a solid tree or a small overhang where she could bring her cubs into the world without fearing they would be washed away. . . .

"Hey!" an unfamiliar voice shrieked from high above Orchid's head. She looked up, gasping as the rain blinded her for a moment. "Look, pandas!" Orchid blinked away the water and saw, clinging to the wavering branches of the trees, a cluster of bedraggled shapes with long tails. Golden monkeys, about ten of them—perhaps all that was left of their troop. They were peering down at Orchid and Root, their strange blue faces contorted in anger around their snub noses, lips peeled back to bare their sharp teeth.

"This is your fault!" one screamed over the sound of the rain, pointing a long finger down at the pandas. "You were supposed to warn us!"

"We didn't know!" Orchid shouted back.

"Where's your Dragon Speaker?" demanded another monkey. Orchid tensed as they started to climb down the trunks of the trees, slowly at first but then faster, leaping from trunk to trunk as if they were so angry they no longer cared if they slipped and fell. "Why didn't he tell us what was going to happen?"

"It's not Sunset's fault," Root growled, slowly shifting his position in the mud, stepping between the advancing monkeys and Orchid. "The Great Dragon didn't say anything about this."

*But that's a lie,* Orchid thought desperately. *Or, at least, we don't know it's the truth.*

*Where* is *Sunset Deepwood?*

"Tenderfoot is dead," one of the monkeys wailed. She had reached the ground and now stood there, tail whipping behind her. "Fleetheart is dead. So many dead . . ."

"And it's all because the pandas let it happen," growled another monkey. "They did this to us. From now on, we listen to no panda! Get them!"

"Run!" Root barked, as the monkeys splashed through the mud toward them. Orchid turned and fixed her gaze back on the rock shelf. If she could make it there, if she had somewhere to plant her paws, then let the monkeys come—she could snap them between her teeth, if only she could keep her grip.

She looked back, and a wave of horror washed over her as she saw that Root was not following her.

"Root, no!" she barked. But Root faced the monkeys down, snarling as they leaped. He got the tail of one between his teeth and tossed it several bear-lengths away with a hard shake of his head. But as soon as he had, more monkeys piled onto his back, getting their grabbing hands into his fur, his ears, biting and scratching. Orchid prepared to run back to him, but then Root's paws slipped. The moment stretched out for what seemed like forever: Root still twisting in the mud even as he fell, trying to free himself from the monkeys' grasp.

The troop sprang away from him as he tumbled, but Root couldn't stop himself. He hit the cliff edge, just like the bamboo had. The impact was sickening, even from so far away. Root rolled and toppled and fell into the floodwater. For a moment a flash of black and white bobbed on the surface, and then he was gone.

Orchid let out a roar of grief, but the crashing of the rain all around her swallowed the sound.

She almost hoped that the monkeys would turn on her, that she would be able to take a few of them down before she fell too—but the monkeys had gone quiet, gathering back in the high branches. Before she knew it, they were gone, and she was left there all alone.

*Not alone.*

Was it Root's voice that broke through her shock, or her own, or something else? Wherever it came from, it was right. Orchid would only be alone if she didn't save her cubs. She had to reach that ledge.

The climb was hard, but she couldn't stop moving. Root needed her to make it. Her cubs needed her.

When her claws finally found solid rock and she pulled herself up onto the jagged path at the top of the ledge, her legs were shaking so hard she almost collapsed right there. But just ahead she saw something that made her heart sing with painful relief. There was a cave. It looked deep and solid, set into the heart of the mountain peak. New energy rose in her muscles, and she hurried to sniff the entrance. It wasn't dry—nothing in the Bamboo Kingdom was dry now; maybe it never would be again—but it was sheltered from the lashing rain. It would be warmer. It would be *safe*.

She hurried inside, going as deep as she could before it was too dim to see. The worn stone under her paws felt calming. This would be a place for the cubs to be born.

*But . . .*

Deep inside the cave, there was a scent. Something that made Orchid's skin crawl. Blood and torn flesh.

This was the lair of a predator.

The light in the cave dimmed even more, and Orchid spun around. Something had passed in front of the entrance. Something bigger than a panda. Its silhouette almost blotted out the faint gray light of the sky outside.

Orchid crouched, baring her teeth. She would protect her cubs, no matter what this creature was—and as her eyes adjusted, she realized it was something she had never seen before. Huge, with giant paws and a long tail, but not round like a bear or thick-furred like a leopard. It was sleek. Two enormous green eyes gleamed in a face of black and orange stripes.

The beast stepped into the cave.

# CHAPTER ONE

LEAF ROLLED OVER AND stretched her paws out in front of her, raking the thin soil with her claws, then rolled again onto her back and slowly opened her eyes. The sky above was a soft gleaming gray, pale and unmarked by clouds. All she could see was the very top of one tall tree at the edge of her vision. Leaf felt almost as if she could tumble into the sky.

Her stomach rumbled.

*There'll be time for sky-gazing after the First Feast,* she thought, letting out a huge yawn and flopping back onto her stomach again. She got to her paws and loped over to the big tree and scratched the back of her ears against its gnarled trunk.

Through the sparse trees that grew on the northern slopes, she could see Aunt Plum and all the other Slenderwoods rising from comfy piles of leaves and clambering down from flat rocks, heading over to the thin bamboo stalks that pushed up between the trees. Leaf shook herself and padded toward the place where she had seen some growing the night before. Sure enough, every few paw-lengths she was able to break off a bunch of tender shoots with thin green leaves sprouting. But she stopped before she had gathered them all.

*Greedy cub now, hungry cub later,* Aunt Plum always said, and she was right.

Leaf held the bunch of shoots tightly in one paw and hurried across the forest floor to the big clearing. The other Slenderwood pandas had all gathered there already, each sitting with their back to a tree, a respectful distance away from one another.

"Come along, Leaf," said Plum, with a yawn. "The Great Dragon won't wait for you."

She said that a lot too. Leaf grinned and sat down at the base of the same tree as little Cane and his mother, Hyacinth. Cane wriggled on his stomach toward the small pile of shoots in front of Hyacinth, but she gently reached out a paw and rolled him away.

"Not quite yet, little one," she said. Cane squeaked in disappointment, and Leaf knew how he felt. The bamboo in her paws smelled delicious, but no panda could begin to eat before the blessing.

Aunt Plum scratched her back against the tree trunk and cleared her throat. "Great Dragon," she said, holding her own shoots out in one paw. "At the Feast of Gray Light your humble pandas bow before you. Thank you for the gift of the bamboo, and the wisdom you bestow upon us."

Leaf bowed her head, and so did all the other pandas in the clearing, including Cane, who dropped his muzzle until his nose rested on the forest floor. There was a short pause before they all looked up again, and the sound of happy crunching filled the clearing. Leaf brought her bamboo to her nose, smelling the fresh, cool scent, and then started to pick off the leaves. She formed them into a small bundle before chomping down on the tasty green ends. Hyacinth stripped the tougher bark from the outside of her bamboo, and passed the softer green shreds from the inside down to Cane, who gobbled them up with gusto.

"The Dragon could be a bit more generous with his gifts," one of the older pandas grumbled, his mouth full of bamboo splinters.

"And you could be more grateful for what you have, Juniper Slenderwood," said Plum, eyeing him sternly through the pawful of green leaves.

"Juniper *Shallowpool*," Juniper muttered.

"There is no shallow pool now, Juniper," said Hyacinth gently. "We're all Slenderwoods now."

"Yeah, if you won't be a Slenderwood, you ought to be *Deepriver*, or *Floodwater*," said Grass, with a snide look over her shoulder toward the edge of the river. Juniper got to his paws with a huff and turned his back on the other pandas, settling on the other side of his tree and chewing on the woody stems of his First Feast.

Leaf watched him with a pinched feeling growing in her heart. That was mean of Grass. Juniper was a crotchety old panda, but she couldn't exactly blame him—she couldn't imagine what it would be like to have her home there one day and vanished the next, swallowed up by the rising river. She had never known any home but the Slenderwood, with its tall, wavering trees and sparse bamboo.

"All of you are stuck in the past," Grass snorted, rolling over onto her back and licking her muzzle. "Nine times a day we thank the Great Dragon for feeding us, but why? Who has seen so much as a dragon-shaped cloud since the flood? Juniper's right—the Dragon has abandoned us."

"Not what I said," grumbled Juniper, without turning around.

Leaf turned to look at Plum, and so did several of the others. Leaf half expected her to snap at Grass, but she just shook her head.

"That isn't how it works, Grass," she said calmly. "The Dragon cannot abandon us. The Great Dragon *is* the Bamboo Kingdom. As long as there are pandas, and there is bamboo to feed us, the Dragon is watching over us." She held up the next long stem of her feast, as if that settled the matter. For a while there was silence, only broken by crunching.

"Do you remember that summer," Crabapple put in, using a long black claw to pick a bamboo shoot out of his teeth, "before the flood, when Juniper's pool dried up? The Dragon Speaker warned us all. You found a deeper pool in plenty of time—remember that, Juniper?"

Juniper just grunted again, but Hyacinth smiled to herself as she nudged a pawful of leaves toward Cane. "Oh, remember the time with the sand foxes?" she said. "Old Oak Cragsight had to take the message to them by foot, right up to the White Spine peaks. Only just made it in time to warn them about the avalanche."

"I thought it was a blizzard?" said Grass, her cynical expression melting a little.

"No, it was an avalanche," grumbled Vinca, wriggling his back against the tree to scratch between his shoulder blades. "*Beware the white wave*—that was the Speaker's message. I remember it distinctly."

Leaf wriggled onto her back again, trying to take her time over the last mouthfuls of her feast. Once they started on this topic, the older pandas could go for hours—they would still be here reminiscing when it was time for the Feast of Golden Light, and the Feast of Sun Climb after that.

Leaf knew that Plum was right, that the Great Dragon was still out there, watching over them. She believed it, truly, she did. But when Plum and the others told their stories of the time before the flood, when the river had been calm and narrow enough to cross, the bamboo plentiful, and every panda had had enough food and space to have their own territory, Leaf couldn't help wondering why things weren't like that anymore.

Oak Cragsight would have gone to the sacred spot on his territory and received the Dragon Speaker's message about the danger to the foxes, as all the pandas would have. That was how Plum said it had worked—the Great Dragon would send its prophecies to the Speaker, and the Speaker would pass them on to the other pandas, who would spread the word of the Dragon to all the other creatures of the Bamboo Kingdom. The pandas were special, the Dragon's chosen messengers.

But still, not one of them had known about the flood until it was upon them. Why had the old ways failed? Had the Great Dragon not warned the Dragon Speaker, or had the Speaker known and just not warned the other pandas?

"What do you think happened to the Dragon Speaker?" Leaf said. She knew it was a question without a real answer—no panda knew where Sunset Deepwood had gone.

"I think it's obvious," said Vinca with a heavy sigh. "It's been a year, and we must face the truth: Speaker Sunset must have died in the flood."

Leaf expected at least some of the other pandas to disagree with him, but to her dismay none of them did. Even Aunt Plum hung her head in quiet grief.

"I met him once," said Hyacinth. "I was only a cub, but I'll always remember how he talked to me as if I were a full-grown panda. He told me that one day I would see the signs too, and maybe I'd be the one to stop an illness from spreading or save a nest or . . . He made it sound as if I could be a hero."

"He was one of the wisest Dragon Speakers," said Plum softly.

"But if Sunset is dead," asked Grass, "why hasn't a new Speaker been chosen? Unless we truly have angered the Dragon so much that it's left us all alone."

Plum shook her head. "We must not lose faith. The Dragon

will send us a new Speaker when the time is right."

The silence that followed this was gloomy. Leaf suspected that all the Slenderwood pandas were asking themselves the same question: *How much longer?*

Leaf got up and shook herself from head to tail. The feast was over, and she didn't really want to stay here and chew over the past any longer.

"I'm going to find Dasher," she announced.

"If you're away for the Feast of Golden Light, don't forget—" Aunt Plum began.

"I'll do the blessing," Leaf reassured her. She trotted across the clearing and bumped her nose against the older panda's cheek as she passed. "Don't worry."

As soon as she was out of the clearing and on her way, Leaf felt a weight lift from her shoulders. So there was no Dragon Speaker—that didn't mean life was all bad. She still had Aunt Plum, and she had her friends, too.

She walked for a few minutes until she'd left the Slenderwood and entered Goldleaf, the territory of the red pandas. There was very little bamboo here, but the trees grew thicker and sturdier.

Leaf sniffed at the trunks she passed for any sign of Dasher, but before she caught the scent of her friends, she heard their voices above her. She looked up. The branches of the trees were shaking as small flashes of red and black ran along them, laughing and hiding between the leaves.

"Dasher!" Leaf called up. One of the red creatures looked down, draping himself over a branch so his head was upside down and his tail dangled over the other side.

"Leaf! Come up here!" cried Dasher Climbing Far. Two more red panda faces also appeared in the thick canopy.

"Hi, Leaf!"

"Come on up, Leaf!"

Leaf grinned up at them and turned to sniff the trunk of the closest tree. It would do nicely. She was so much bigger than her red-panda friends that she had to be a bit more careful where she put her paws, but once Leaf Slenderwood started to climb, there was no panda in the Northern Forest who could match her. She quickly found purchase, digging her claws into the bark, and began to climb the tree, lifting herself up onto one branch and then using a thick knot as a paw hold to stretch across to the next. Soon enough she was high above the ground, and then she was in the canopy itself, where the swaying of the trees was enough to make a less sure-footed creature panic. The first sunlight glimmered through the leaves, lighting the world around her in green and gold.

"We're going to climb the Grandfather Gingko! Race to the very top," said Jumper Climbing Far as Leaf pulled herself up onto the same thick branch as the red pandas. "Ready?"

Chomper Digging Deep shook her head. "That's not fair to Leaf," she said. "She's just climbed a whole tree while you've been sitting on your butt eating acorns!"

"Well, that just gives you two a fighting chance—right, Leaf?" Dasher said, turning on the spot, his deft little paws dancing on the thick branch.

"Right!" Leaf huffed. "I'm ready when you are!"

"Go!" squeaked Jumper, and he and Chomper both took off, giggling to themselves as they leaped to another branch.

Dasher and Leaf exchanged a grin.

"Let's get them!" Dasher waved his tail and charged off, and Leaf followed him. She knew she couldn't go as fast or jump as far as her red-panda friends, but that didn't matter—she could see that the other two had hastily run out onto a branch that was too short and would have to turn around, whereas Leaf's more considered approach would always get her where she needed to go.

The Grandfather Gingko was the tallest tree in the whole Northern Forest, towering above the rest of the canopy like a bright golden sunrise. She made for it, sticking carefully to the thickest branches, hugging the trunks, and pulling herself higher and higher. She almost slipped when she accidentally put her back paw into a hollow where a jay was nesting. The bird squawked and pecked at her paw pads. Leaf gasped and slid a little way back down the trunk, and as she did she looked down and saw a long, long fall down to the ground below her . . . but she used her claws to dig in, slow, and stop her slide.

"Sorry!" she said to the jay as she climbed up again, careful not to put any paws inside its nest this time. The jay just chattered at her and puffed up its smoke-gray neck feathers in disgust.

The last ascent to the top of the gingko tree was one of the trickiest bits of climbing in the forest, but Leaf had made it before, and the Grandfather tree only seemed to get taller and stronger every time. She knew just which branches to follow to the very top. Dasher was right by her side, clinging on to the thin twigs that would snap under Leaf's paws, and the other two red pandas weren't far behind. Leaf pulled herself up onto the crook of the tallest branches and settled there in triumph, catching her breath as she looked out through the gold leaves and down to the forest below.

The Northern Forest surrounded the tree, its patches of tall and strong trunks broken up by thinner places like the Slenderwood clearing, where the bamboo grew in sparse clumps. Beyond the trees, she could see down into the valley where the river ran, so wide that no creature could swim across. Its swift and dangerous currents made ripples that looked like shimmering snakes—or dragons—as the sun rose.

Beyond the river was the Southern Forest. Its slopes were just as steep as on Leaf's side, but where the Northern Forest was gray and sparse, the trees there looked lush and green. Even from so far away, if Leaf stared for a long time she thought she could see bamboo growing in enormous bushes, so big that even the hungriest panda couldn't eat it all.

The thought of the bamboo made her stomach rumble, and she licked her muzzle as she looked up at the rising sun. It was time for the Feast of Golden Light. She had no bamboo, but she couldn't miss a feast, so she cast around until she found a cluster of small yellow fruits hanging from one of the gingko branches. They were nowhere near as tasty as bamboo, but they would have to do. She picked one and held it in her paws as she hung her head.

"Great Dragon, at the Feast of Golden Light your humble

panda bows before you," she said. "Thank you for the gift of the bamboo—I mean, this stinky yellow fruit—and the strength you bestow upon us."

The red pandas sat in the branches around her, swinging their tails as she took a bite of the fruit, tearing through the soft yellow flesh to the crunchy nut hiding inside. It really wasn't much compared to bamboo, but the important thing was to eat something.

"I heard Scrabbler saying the river's calmed down a bit since the last rain," said Jumper, once she had swallowed all of the fruit she could bear to eat.

"Really?" Leaf's ears pricked up and she peered down the northern slope toward the glistening water again. It still looked to her like the currents were very fast, but maybe, maybe this would be the time . . .

"Well . . . Scrab says a lot of things," Dasher said. "He's probably imagining it."

"We're going to do it," Leaf said firmly. "Maybe not today, but we'll get across. I believe we will."

"Not going to be so much about believing as swimming," said Jumper, dangling upside down from his branch. "Can you swim?"

"I can!" Leaf snorted. *Not . . . brilliantly,* she added to herself. *Not like I can climb. But we'll find a way!*

"Do you really think they're over there?" Dasher asked, a hint of skepticism in his voice. "Your mother and your twin?"

Leaf stared at the Southern Forest until its deep green trunks began to blur and swim in front of her eyes.

"Yes," she said. "That's what Aunt Plum always told me. She said her sister Orchid came to her with two cubs—she asked Plum to keep me safe, and then she left with the other one. Where else could they have gone?"

The red pandas didn't answer her, and Leaf was glad. She knew, obviously, that it was possible that they weren't in the Southern Forest at all—that, apart from Plum, all her family had gone the same way as Sunset Deepwood.

But she refused to believe it, not while there was a whole forest just over the shimmering water.

"One day, Dasher," she said again. "We'll cross over the river, and I'll find my family."

# CHAPTER TWO

"I COULDN'T EAT ANOTHER mouthful," said Rain, stretching her paws out in a satisfied yawn. She leaned back against the large bamboo stand, the strong canes creaking as they bent to a more comfortable angle. She looked up and saw a shoot of fresh green leaves poking out from between the large canes, just within reach. *Well, maybe one more mouthful,* she thought, and hooked her claws around it and tore it out.

But before she could crunch down, the bamboo was yanked away from her.

"Hey!" she growled, as the other panda climbed up over her, using her shoulder as a stepping-stone, and settled down on a jut of rock a few bear-lengths up the slope from Rain. Rain got up, snarling, and climbed up after her.

The other panda, Blossom, was just about to stuff the green leaves into her mouth when Rain pulled herself up onto the rock and snapped her jaws down on one end of the cane. "Mmf! That's mine!" she growled through her teeth. "Get your own!"

"You're mistaken, dear," said Blossom, in a sickly sweet tone. "I'm your elder. This cane is mine, and this rock is mine. Why don't *you* get back to the lower slopes with the other cubs? There's plenty of bamboo down there."

Rain growled through her teeth. There *was* plenty of bamboo, but that wasn't the point. She gave a sharp tug on the cane and felt the stiff stem cracking.

"Rain's right—she picked that shoot," said another voice, and Rain looked down to see Pebble climbing through a fork between two trees, his wide face creased in a frown. "I saw you take it."

Blossom's condescending smirk faded and she curled her paws tighter around the bamboo cane. Rain snarled again and gave it another yank. It creaked for a moment and then snapped in two. Rain lost her footing and slid gracelessly back down the rocks, landing with a thump in the carpet of leaves at the bottom. But as she got back to her paws, she huffed in satisfaction. She had all the juiciest leaves on her half, and Blossom was left with the woody, crunchy stem.

"What disrespect!" Blossom spat.

"Yeah, you're right!" Rain shot back. "I don't respect you, not one bit!"

"Rain!" snapped another voice, and this time Rain's hackles smoothed and she turned slowly. Her mother, Peony, was standing behind her. "Apologize to Blossom."

"I will not," Rain muttered. "She's a thief, Mother. She thinks just because she's older—"

"*Rain,*" Peony said again, a hint of a warning growl vibrating in her chest. "Apologize."

Rain sagged. She looked up at Blossom, who had shifted on the rock so her back was almost completely turned to Rain, as if she was deeply offended—though she was still peeking over her shoulder. Rain's muzzle twisted in annoyance; then she drew herself up.

"Sorry, Blossom," she said, in a clear and calm voice. Then she flashed the older panda a grin, stuffed the pawful of tasty green bamboo leaves into her mouth, and chewed hard, fixing her eyes on Blossom's until the delicious plant was all gone. Blossom snorted and flopped down on her rock. Behind her, Rain heard both Peony and Pebble sigh.

"Walk with me, both of you," Peony said, twitching her ears at Pebble. Rain followed her mother, her paw steps light with smugness, and her best friend fell in just behind.

They followed the well-trodden path as it wound down the hill, the smoothest and shallowest way to the river. It would have been quicker to take the steeper slopes in a sort of barely controlled tumble, using the bamboo and trees to catch herself when she slipped. But she was already a little sore from her fall off Blossom's rock, so she dutifully followed behind Peony instead.

"What have I told you, Rain?" her mother said as they padded steadily down, passing through a gap in the rocks between lush green curtains of ivy.

"Not to swim out into the middle of the river," Rain said. "And not to fall asleep with my mouth open."

Peony shook her head. "Life will be much easier if you try to get along with the others," she said.

"I do get along," Rain said. "I get along with Pebble, don't I? And Horizon. And the little cubs are all right."

Peony reached a flat space where the path passed by a fallen tree trunk and climbed up to sit on it. She sat and scratched behind her ear with her forepaw. "Rain, there are over *twenty* pandas living on the Prosperhill now. In the old days . . . Move out of the way, Pebble; there's a good boy."

Rain turned and saw another panda coming up the path. As if to prove Peony's point, Mist Prosperhill's thin fur almost brushed Rain's as she passed by, and Pebble had to take a few steps into the undergrowth to get out of the way.

"Good Long Light, Peony," the old panda croaked as she passed.

"And to you," said Peony with a short bow of her head.

She waited until Mist had gone farther up the hill before she carried on with her lecture. "Things weren't always like this. Before the flood, we never would have lived all together like this. Pandas like Blossom aren't used to having to share— they wouldn't have had to see another panda for seasons at a time if they didn't want to."

"Well, she's had my entire lifetime to get used to it," Rain huffed.

"And you've had a lifetime to get used to her." Peony sighed. "It won't be long until the Feast of Sun Fall. Don't you both have chores to be getting on with? I'm sure the nests could do with some fresh reeds before Moon Climb."

Rain knew her mother was changing the subject, but she didn't mind. That just meant Rain had won the argument.

"Come on," said Pebble. "Let's fetch the cubs and go get some reeds."

"Be back for the feast," Peony said, lying down on the trunk and shutting her eyes.

Rain snorted, and she and Pebble carried on down the worn path through the undergrowth, side by side until they came to the flat, sheltered place where Horizon and Dawn were sitting—the two friends getting along perfectly well without stealing anybody's bamboo, Rain noted. Their young cubs, Frog and Fir, were tumbling and rolling around at their feet. Frog was the older one, but he always let Fir win.

They were both content to join Rain and Pebble on a trip to the river, and they bounced happily along the path just ahead of them until Rain suddenly stopped, her paws slipping slightly on the dewy ground.

"Wait!" she gasped, and sank to her belly. Frog and Fir spun around and bounced back up the slope to her, their black eyes wide with concern. "It's . . . I'm . . . I'm getting . . . a *vision!*"

Rain rolled over onto her back and stared up at the sky, letting her jaw fall open.

"What is it?" Frog yelped.

"What can you see?" Fir tried to put her paws up on Rain's belly, and she swatted her away.

"Silence! It's the Great Dragon! Speak to me, O Great One . . ."

The cubs crouched down in front of her, their upside-down faces trembling with excitement. Out of the corner of her eye she could also see Pebble, sitting still a little way off, but she ignored him.

"The Dragon says . . . it says . . . that I mustn't go to the river! Terrible things will happen if I go to the river today! Oh, and Pebble too, he can't go either. The Dragon says you two must fetch the reeds by yourselves!"

Rain let her legs go limp and rolled onto her side, closing her eyes and panting for a moment. Then she got unsteadily to her paws and looked down at the little cubs, frowning in concern.

"Oh, but how can I let you two fetch the reeds all alone? Are you big enough or strong enough to do it? Perhaps I should ignore the Dragon's warning. . . ."

"No!" Fir practically screamed. "Me and Frog can do it— we're *so* strong. Aren't we?"

"We'll get so many reeds," Frog agreed, springing to his paws. "The Dragon will be really proud of us!"

"I'm sure it will," said Rain gently as the two cubs turned and sprinted down the slope at full speed, like a couple of tiny, fluffy rocks rolling downhill.

Rain turned to Pebble and gave him a wide-jawed grin. Pebble rolled his eyes, but he chuckled too.

"Frog's almost too old for that, you know," he said. "One day he'll see through you, and then you'll have to start doing all your own chores again."

"Nah," said Rain. "Anyway, by then Yew will have had her

cub and I can start training him to believe it too."

"Is this what pandas have come to, then?" said a sneering voice from above her head. She looked up and saw a big golden monkey hanging from a branch by its tail, swinging from side to side. It picked at its left ear, which had a nasty-looking tear in it, and pulled a scornful face.

"Go away, rot-breath," Rain snapped back.

The monkey ignored her. It picked a piece of fruit from the branch near its head, sniffed at it, and then hurled it into the bushes. "Didn't the whole Bamboo Kingdom look up to you pandas, once upon a time? Weren't you *important*? Such a shame the Great Dragon stopped talking to you. What do you think you did to make it angry? Doesn't matter, I suppose. Nobody's ever going to listen to your stupid blotchy faces again."

"Nobody ever listened to *your* weird blue faces to begin with," Rain retorted. "Who cares what a monkey thinks about anything? Now, *I'm* going to go down to the river for a swim. Coming?" she said to Pebble.

"Why not?" said Pebble, and they both turned their backs on the monkey and walked away into the undergrowth. Rain heard it laughing behind them, but neither of them looked back.

After a while they had put a thick line of trees between them and the annoying monkey, and they came to a jut of rock where they could see down to the edge of the fast-running river. Rain watched the Long Light sun sparkle on the water, and her fur prickled with the urge to leap in and splash around.

She turned to tell Pebble that she'd race him into the water, but then she stopped. Pebble was looking out over the river too, but his face was thoughtful, and a little sad.

"What's up?" she said.

"That monkey's right, you know." Pebble sighed. "Things were better when we had a Dragon Speaker. All the animals in the Bamboo Kingdom looked up to us. We had a purpose."

"I suppose it would be nice to be able to tell creatures like that monkey what to do," Rain agreed. "But Pebble—it's not *real*. I mean, this whole story about a Great Dragon who comes down and tells one panda all about what's going to happen. There's no way that's a real thing."

Pebble cocked his head at Rain. "You really don't believe in the Great Dragon?"

Rain stretched her front paws out until her back gave a satisfying click. "I don't know. Maybe. But there's certainly no Dragon Speaker now, and we're still doing all right. There's plenty of bamboo, and gullible cubs to do things for us. Who needs more than that? Being the mouthpiece of some great powerful sky dragon sounds too much like hard work to me."

Pebble hesitated, still lost in thought. Rain nudged him in the shoulder with her nose.

"Seriously, who cares if there's a Dragon Speaker or not? The important thing is that Frog thinks there is, and I'm it! Now come on. Last one to the river's a stinky gingko!"

This finally got a laugh out of Pebble, and Rain jumped down off the rock and loped down the slope to the water with her friend's paws thudding just behind her.

She ran over the tangle of rocks and roots and stones that made up the bank and plunged into the river with a happy snort. The water lapped over her muzzle, cooling and fresh. There was a huge splash behind her as Pebble landed in the shallows and slapped the water with his forepaws.

Rain's mother was right about the river—it was dangerous to swim out too far.

It hadn't always been like this. Peony had told Rain many stories of the way the kingdom used to be, before the flood had swelled the river to such a vast size that the lowest hills were completely underwater. Whole territories had vanished. When the rain came, pandas had tried to climb tall trees to escape the water, and they'd been trapped there or had had to swim for their lives from the top branches and been dragged under by the terrible currents.

But that was a year ago. Rain had grown up with the river as it was now, and she knew all the rivulets and shallows as well as she knew her own fur pattern. In some places there were smooth, stony banks, and in other places trees and rocks that used to be on dry land stuck up out of the water, breaking up the flow. A careful panda could swim happily around them without getting too close to the dangerous currents that flowed near the middle of the river.

Rain took a deep breath, and dived.

Under the water, there was a whole different world. Rocks and roots covered with soft green algae housed tiny glittering silver fish and turtles with gleaming opal shells.

It was calm, but a little creepy, too. The water was clear,

but there were no smells or sounds, so everything felt soft and slightly unreal. Rain used her big paws to push herself along under the surface, nosing at the underwater branches sticking up from the silt riverbed. A flash of orange, gold, and black over her head made her look up to see a shoal of carp, circling in the sunlight.

She surfaced again and gasped for breath. She had swum out into the faster flow of the river, and she could see Pebble sitting on a rock near the shore, watching her anxiously as she floated away from him. She snorted. He had nothing to worry about. She was the best swimmer in the Prosperhill, and she knew exactly how far she could go without being dragged away. She dived again, swimming hard for the shore, and a moment later she burst from the water right next to Pebble's rock.

"Worried?" she asked, putting her paws up on the rock to steady herself. But Pebble wasn't looking at her anymore—he was staring at the bank. His muzzle twitched as he sniffed the air.

Rain tried to sniff too, but her nose was still full of the scents of the river, fish and wet moss. Before she could ask Pebble what he was sniffing at, she heard the voice of a panda—first one, and then several. Horizon and Dawn, she thought, and Frog, too.

"A new panda!" they were saying.

"A *new* panda?" Rain echoed. She was sure they couldn't mean it—it was too soon for the new cub to be born, and there were no other pandas living anywhere nearby.

"Come on, let's go and see what they're talking about!" Pebble jumped down into the shallows and they splashed together toward the shore. It wasn't hard to find the source of the commotion—by the time they had climbed the hill, all the Prosperhill pandas had crowded themselves onto one flat ledge overlooking the panda path.

"What's happening?" Rain asked Peony. Her mother looked at her with flat surprise.

"Can't you scent it? There's an outsider approaching. Or at least . . . they smell familiar, somehow. But it's not a Prosperhill panda. I'm certain of that."

Rain sniffed again, but it was hard to pick out a single panda's scent when the rest of them were crowded around her, shifting excitedly from paw to paw. She managed to wiggle through the group to the edge of the rock, just in time to see a shape emerge from between the trees below.

It was a large, fluffy black-and-white shape—unmistakably an adult male panda. His fur was a little thin with age, and across one of his haunches he had a large scar. But his steps were as firm and strong as the trunks of trees. He had exceptionally large eye markings, and he stopped as he came onto the path and looked up at the assembled pandas, blinking as an expression of joy settled across his features.

"My dear pandas," he said. "I have found you at last."

This meant absolutely nothing to Rain, but all around her a cry began to go up from the older pandas, a whisper at first and then a roar.

"Is that Sunset?"

"It's Sunset!"

"Sunset Deepwood!"

Rain sat back on her haunches and was left alone on the rock as the other pandas rushed down the slope, crying out their greetings.

"You're alive! You've returned to us!"

"The Dragon Speaker has returned!"

# CHAPTER THREE

GHOST BORN OF WINTER made no sound as he padded
through the snow, across the wide open ridge of the White
Spine Mountains. Up ahead, his littermates Frost and Snowstorm were sleek, dappled shadows darting from rock to rock,
pausing to sniff the air or poke their whiskers into a hole in
the ground. Ghost sniffed around too, but he couldn't scent
any prey on the icy wind.

He glanced back and paused for a second to let Shiver
catch up. His sister was the runt of the litter, and her legs were
shorter and her fur thinner than the others, so she always
had to run in scampering bursts, stopping to catch her breath
often.

"Have they found anything yet?" she whispered as she
reached him, shaking the snow off her whiskers. Her spotted
head barely reached Ghost's shoulder.

"Not yet," he replied.

"Well, maybe we'll find one first!" Shiver said brightly. She closed her eyes. "Snow Cat, show us your paw prints!"

She opened her eyes and looked around, as if she were expecting to literally see the prints of the Snow Cat leading her to a burrow full of tasty prey.

"Let's catch up with the other two," Ghost suggested. Shiver nodded, and they advanced across the snowfield. Despite the size difference, their paces were well matched, with Shiver's frequent pauses for breath and Ghost's slower, heavier tread.

Snowstorm and Frost had paused in the lee of a large rock, and Ghost saw Snowstorm turn to look back at them, her tail lashing and ears pricked. She'd found something.

*Wait for us,* Ghost thought. *We're all supposed to be hunting together. . . .*

He put on a burst of speed, but Snowstorm and Frost had already moved on, creeping around the rock and out of sight.

"Mother said they're not . . . supposed to go too far ahead," Shiver panted.

Ghost simply nodded. Winter had told them to stick together, and with very good reason. They *all* needed to get hunting practice if they were ever going to be able to make the leap across the Endless Maw, become adults, and finally move out of their mother's den.

He glanced up at the towering peaks that rose from the ridge to the north, black and white against the swirling snow. There had been another avalanche only a few nights ago. They'd been safe in their den, but they'd all heard the cracking and rumbling of the white waves of snow as they rolled down the mountain. It was a wonder there were any prey animals left living among the White Spines—but then, Ghost supposed they were just like him and the other snow leopards. They didn't want to leave the place they'd always called home.

Ghost and Shiver hurried around the rock and found Snowstorm and Frost on the other side of it. Snowstorm flicked her tail at them again.

"See it?" she hissed. "Right there!"

Ghost peered through the snow, and, sure enough, there was a flicker of brown beside a pile of gray rocks, half buried in a snowdrift. The brown ears of a mountain hare. It was large and tough-looking.

"We should sneak around and pounce from the rocks," Frost said, and set off at a fast creep, his body so low to the ground he left a trail of disturbed snow behind. Ghost tried to follow him, but his broader shoulders and stocky legs made it hard to slink. So instead he focused on staying quiet, placing his paws carefully, and letting the snow muffle his movement.

Shiver raced ahead, but she couldn't catch up with her faster littermates, who had already circled around in a wide arc and begun to climb up the rock on silent paws. The hare never saw or heard them coming. They sprang, first Snowstorm and then Frost, and trapped the creature under their paws. But the hare was surprisingly strong, and it wriggled and kicked in their grip. Its powerful back leg struck Frost under the chin, sending him reeling back.

"Ugh! Stay still, you little—Ghost, come and help me!"

Snowstorm growled through a mouthful of writhing fur. Ghost put his head down and charged toward them. He might not have been very good at stealth and speed, but it felt good to unleash his power. He put a heavy paw down on the hare to hold it still, and finished it off with one clean, powerful bite to the back of the neck, just like Winter had taught him.

"We did it!" Shiver panted, catching up behind them. Ghost saw Snowstorm and Frost exchange a look, and hoped they wouldn't say anything mean to their sister. Shiver would have been able to catch her own prey if they'd let her go first instead of rushing off ahead.

"Let's eat," Frost said instead, licking his lips. "Mother said we should eat if we caught something."

Snowstorm reared back and batted playfully at the air around his ears. "Not yet, stupid. We've got to thank the Snow Cat first."

Shiver sat down between them and kneaded the snow with her paws. "We thank the Snow Cat for giving us this prey," she began, and the other three leopards joined in.

"May you leave your paw prints in the snow, that we may follow them," they said together.

Snowstorm, Frost, and Shiver immediately fell upon the hare and tucked in, delighted. Ghost knew he needed to eat too. They often went for several days without fresh prey, and his stomach was rumbling at the idea of feeling full again. He tore mouthfuls of stringy flesh from the hare and gobbled them down as quickly as he could.

For a while there were no sounds but the chewing and

purring of four hungry cubs, and even those were muffled by the falling snow.

Then a yowl split the air behind them. Ghost spun around, kicking up a flurry around his paws, and saw two spotted shapes emerging from behind another rock. Two more leopard cubs, a little younger than Ghost and his littermates. His heart sank as he recognized them.

"Look, Sleet," one of them said. "It's the freaks Born of Winter."

Ghost let out a rumbling growl as Brisk and Sleet Born of Icebound padded toward them.

"This isn't your territory," Frost snarled, licking his muzzle. "Get out of here, or we'll make you."

"Ooh, are you going to set your freak brother on us?" Brisk tilted her head. "Or your weak little sister?"

Shiver started to stalk toward them, her teeth bared. "Try me!" she growled.

"Is Ghost even here?" Sleet mewed, turning around in fake confusion while still casting mean looks right at Ghost. "Where is the big white-furred weirdo?"

Ghost tried to ignore Sleet's teasing, but he couldn't help feeling self-conscious, treading the snow uneasily with his perfectly white paws. He knew there was nothing wrong with being larger than his littermates, or with having no spots, but Sleet and Brisk certainly seemed to think there was.

"That's it." Snowstorm leaped, bounding right over Ghost's back to land in the snow in front of Brisk and Sleet. "I'm going to make you pay for that."

Ghost and Frost hurried to back her up, and Ghost opened his jaws and let his deep growl out as a roar. Brisk and Sleet both flinched, and Snowstorm and Frost joined in with the roar as they advanced on the two cubs Born of Icebound.

Ghost felt a flush of warmth envelop him as he stood side by side with his littermates, and Brisk and Sleet began to back off.

"What, don't you want to fight?" Shiver snapped.

"What kind of cowards are you?" Frost backed her up.

"Afraid to face a family of freaks?" Ghost leaped, jaws open, and snapped his teeth together just a few paw-lengths short of Brisk's nose. The cub whimpered, and the two littermates slid and scrambled back, turned tail, and fled across the snowfield.

"Yeah, don't come back here!" Shiver yelled after them.

Snowstorm shook her head. "They're such idiots."

"If they wanted our hare, they shouldn't have announced themselves," Frost said, behind Ghost. "They should have crept up on us . . . like *this*!"

Ghost ducked, but just slightly too late. Frost tumbled over his shoulders and landed on his back in the snow, but his paws still held on to Ghost's thick neck, and he pulled Ghost's head down and landed a playful gnaw on his ear.

Ghost reared up in mock fury. "Then we would have had them just where we wanted them!" He brought his paws down and batted at Frost's exposed stomach. He was extra careful not to hit him—Ghost knew his claws didn't pull back like the others, but Winter had taught him how to play safely with his littermates, and Frost didn't flinch as the black talons scraped the air above him.

"Yeah, it'd be four against two!" Shiver said, and pounced on Snowstorm's tail. Snowstorm gave a fake wail of agony and batted Shiver across the back of the head. Shiver fell back, her paws spread exaggeratedly wide, and Snowstorm went in for the kill, pressing her nose into the fluff under her sister's chin, making Shiver giggle and splutter.

The four of them rolled and laughed in the snow, and Ghost felt that warmth spread through him again, even though his paws were getting frozen and the wind whipped fiercely around them. He and Shiver might not be the greatest hunters, but when it came down to it, the cubs Born of Winter would stick together, no matter what.

# CHAPTER FOUR

Rain gripped the long bamboo stems in her jaws. She hurried back up the path, careful not to get them caught on the undergrowth as she climbed between the mossy rocks, threading her way uphill between the trunks of the gingko and pine trees, heading for the feast clearing.

Her mouth watered, but she didn't stop to sneakily eat any of the stems she carried, as she might have done on a different day. Pebble walked behind her, inspecting the bamboo they passed for new shoots that would be perfect to pick for the feast.

Bamboo was being gathered from all over the Prosperhill for this Feast of Dying Light. There would be more than plenty for every panda. Nobody had said that this would be a special feast, but it had just seemed obvious that it was a celebration. Sunset Deepwood was back.

Rain and Pebble passed by Peony, who was drinking from a clear stream that trickled between two rocks, forming a tiny sparkling waterfall. She let some run over her muzzle and then shook her head, spraying droplets into the air. She saw Rain, and ran over to give her an affectionate lick on the ear.

"It's so wonderful," she said. "Everything feels renewed. Can you sense it too? Look there." She pointed with her nose toward a little tussock where new bamboo sprouts were poking up through a layer of moss. "I've seen many of those, since Sunset came back to us. I think the whole Southern Forest is . . . it's as if it's celebrating his return."

Rain nodded, pleased to see her mother so happy. She wasn't quite sure it was true—bamboo often sprang up in odd places, and fast, and there was nothing about this new growth that seemed like a sign to her. But then, she'd been sure there was no Dragon Speaker and never would be again, and now here he was.

*I guess anything is possible.*

"Things will be better now," Peony said. "We'll be connected to the Great Dragon again. With his help, we'll be able to get back to normal, the way things were before the flood."

"Not . . . quite the way they were," said Pebble in a small voice. Peony's eyes turned sad, and she gave Pebble a kind nuzzle against the side of his head.

"No, you're right," she said. "Some things can be made right again, but not all."

Rain looked at the ground. She wished she knew something to say to make Pebble feel better, but she knew there was nothing that could bring his big brother back. Unlike her, Pebble was just about old enough to remember the flood clearly, and the memories were painful.

"Let's get to the clearing," Pebble said, shaking himself from tail to ears. "We can't miss the blessing!"

"Quite right," said Peony gently, and led the way along the path.

The feast clearing was a dip on the peak of one of the steep hills that made up the Southern Forest. It was a clear, grassy space surrounded by trees and rocks. Rain dropped her bamboo in the center and took a helping for herself, then climbed up into the low crook of a tree and made herself comfortable as the rest of the Prosperhill pandas gathered. They climbed up the hill from all directions and took their places in the soft grass or up on the rocks, until they looked a bit like a flock of large, round birds.

From her perch in the tree, Rain turned to look around at the Bamboo Kingdom. The sun was setting at the mouth of the river, leaving half the valley in deep black shadow and the other half ablaze with golden light.

The Southern Forest was a rolling series of forested peaks that climbed higher and higher and eventually vanished into the clouds. Below her to the north was the rushing river and, on the other side of it, the sharp peaks of the Northern Forest and the White Spine Mountains beyond, like a pale reflection of the Southern Forest.

*The world is so big,* Rain thought. *I suppose I could never know for certain that there was really no Dragon anywhere out there.*

Rain felt a little guilty as she watched Sunset Deepwood crest the hill with old Mist beside him. When he'd first appeared, though the air had thrummed with the excitement of the other pandas, she hadn't felt particularly impressed. For a start, her tricks with the cubs wouldn't work anymore. *And she might have to admit to Pebble that she'd been wrong.* She knew it was petty, but it stung a little bit.

Still, she leaned forward curiously as Sunset selected a pawful of bamboo from the pile and sat down in the center of the clearing to wait for the other pandas to settle around him. What would he say? Where had he been?

Finally, a hush fell over the clearing. Usually, one of the oldest male Prosperhill pandas, either Mist or Squall, would say the blessing. But at this feast, neither of them spoke. Sunset seemed to pause politely until it was clear they were all waiting for him, then held up his bamboo and looked to the sky.

"At the Feast of Dying Light, your humble pandas bow before you. Thank you for the gift of the bamboo, and the kindness you bestow upon us."

Normally, the final word would be the sign for the feast clearing to be filled with the crunching and splitting of bamboo as the pandas tucked into their delicious meal, but every panda seemed more hesitant to begin. Even Rain paused a little before she brought the green leaves to her mouth and began slowly to tear them off.

"Go on, eat!" Sunset chuckled. "The Dragon wouldn't want you to go hungry."

At that, the pandas finally started to chomp on their bamboo, though Rain thought many of them were trying to do so more quietly than normal.

"Speaker," said Horizon, pulling a cane apart with her paws for Fir to chew on, "we can't bear the suspense any longer. Won't you tell us your story?"

"Yes, please, Dragon Speaker," said Bay, and several of the other pandas nodded through their mouthfuls of bamboo. Azalea leaned so far forward on her rock she almost toppled over.

"I think I will have to keep to the bare bones of the tale," Sunset said. "It would take another four seasons to relate everything that has happened."

He paused, and the feast clearing seemed to hold its breath.

"I should begin before the flood, but the truth is, before the rains came and the mountains shook, everything was quite ordinary. My brother Dusk and I were walking together when it happened—as we did sometimes, even though his territory was far away. We saw the White Spines crumble and the white wave begin to roll down toward the river. We saw the sky darken and tear itself apart, and the great flood rise up to meet us. We were both caught in it. I saw my brother torn away from me, and he . . ." Sunset paused, hanging his head. "Poor Dusk. He was taken by the river. He drowned."

A chorus of sighs ran through the clearing, and many of the pandas hung their heads and paused their feast. Rain glanced over at Pebble. He was staring at Sunset with wide and liquid eyes, his bamboo apparently forgotten in his lap. Many of them had lost family and friends in the flood, but Sunset's story was so horribly similar to Pebble's. . . .

Sunset closed his eyes for a moment, then opened them.

"I was swept away too, but I didn't drown. I was washed up onshore a long, long way away from here. I didn't know where I was, or what had happened, but I knew that all of you must be suffering—that all of the Bamboo Kingdom was in trouble—and so I set off to try to come back to you. Many adventures and trials lay before me. . . ." He paused to take a big mouthful of bamboo leaves. As soon as he'd finished the sprout he was holding, one of the other pandas rushed forward to take the freshest one left in the pile and present it to him. He thanked them, and chewed thoughtfully for another moment.

"You see, there were many in those times who had been hurt by the flood, and they blamed us. They blamed me. They could not accept that I, too, had had no idea what had been coming. So I was waylaid at every turn. Leopards, a herd of takins, even a flock of crows tried to keep me away from you. The leopards gave me this." He twisted to show off the long, pale scar that broke up the fur across his flank. "Luckily, the Great Dragon gave me the strength to fight them and escape."

He finished the next pawful of bamboo, and Rain saw several of the pandas begin to get to their paws to refill his lap, but Pebble practically flew to the pile in the middle of the clearing and reached Sunset first.

"Thank you, young . . . ?" Sunset said, with a tilt of his head.

"Oh! P-Pebble, Speaker," Pebble gasped.

"Thank you, Pebble."

Rain couldn't help letting a tiny chuckle escape her throat as Pebble bustled back to his own spot. The Dragon Speaker was certainly impressive, with his grand stories of near-death encounters with leopards and everything, but Pebble vibrating with excitement at hearing the panda say his name was pretty silly.

Sunset kept talking, telling stories of long climbs over snowy peaks, fights with small but ferocious manul cats in the deep forest, and many missed feasts in his apparently tireless efforts to return to the Prosperhill. The gathered pandas gasped in all the right places, and some of them even forgot their own bamboo for a moment, they were so wrapped up in the dramatic tale.

Rain ate steadily and thoughtfully.

It was just so strange. Only this Long Light, she had been playing at being a Dragon Speaker for the cubs—well, for her own benefit, but she knew that Frog and Fir enjoyed the drama of her "visions" too. And now, here was a real Speaker. Did that mean that the Dragon was real too? But if there really was a Dragon, and Sunset really had this special connection to it, then why *hadn't* he—he, of all pandas—had some idea that the flood was coming?

Obviously, that stupid blue-faced monkey hadn't been *right* exactly, but . . .

"I think that's enough about me," Sunset said. "More than enough, in fact! All that matters now is that I'm home."

"Quite right," chorused several pandas, and others started

to roar and slap their paws on the ground in agreement.

Sunset held up his paws, and they all fell silent. Rain blinked in surprise, then went back to chewing on her last woody stem. Commanding the Prosperhill pandas to stop their chatter with just a gesture—now *that* would be a great power to have.

"I'm home," Sunset repeated, "with my beloved pandas. And I can see that you are all suffering, as I have suffered. Let me ease your pain. Tell me *your* stories of the flood. I want to hear how each of you survived, and what you lost. That way we will all be able to begin to heal, together."

Rain let out a heavy breath. That sounded like the last thing she'd like to spend her Dying Light doing. Especially because she'd only just been born at the time. What was her story going to be? *I was born. It was wet. I got dry later.*

No, she was going to have to sit here and say nothing while the rest of the pandas recounted the terrible things that had happened to them. She shifted awkwardly in her tree and looked around at the other pandas, who all suddenly looked solemn. Perhaps Sunset was right, and this would make them feel better. She could sit quietly for it, if that was the case.

The first panda to speak up was Cypress. He padded to the edge of his rock and sat looking around at the other pandas.

"Well, um . . . I was in my own territory when it happened, higher up the slopes. The ground shook. I was almost crushed by falling rocks, and then the rain started. . . ."

He went on, talking about the long drop that had broken his paw, and how he had found his way to the Prosperhill after the rains stopped, where the other pandas had helped him rest.

"And what of your family, of other pandas?" Sunset asked.

"My older sister, Citrus, was my only family. I haven't seen her since the flood. I . . . I thought she must be dead," Cypress said. "But perhaps now that you've found us again . . . perhaps . . ."

"Thank you for your story, Cypress," said Sunset. "Who would like to be next to share theirs?"

One by one, each of the pandas stepped forward, except the few like Rain, Frog, and Fir who were too young to remember the flood at all. The stories had a lot in common—slippery falls, dangerous climbs, encounters with panicking animals, fevers that seemed like they would be fatal—or were, in some cases. Rain listened with a heavy heart to stories of missing parents and dead cubs. Pebble and his mother told their story together, describing Stone's death in the terrible tide.

When Peony's turn came, Rain listened intently. Her mother had never really spoken of what had happened to her.

"I was pregnant," she said. "And my mate . . . he died." Peony cleared her throat, and Rain felt a sharp pang of sadness. She had never known her father, and had never really missed him—but it hurt to see how much it still pained Peony to even mention him. "I thought there was no way I could escape, but I kept climbing, higher and higher. And after the flood, my beautiful Rain came to me," she added, shooting a fond glance up at Rain in her tree. "Safe and sound."

Sunset shook his head. "It must have been so hard," he said.

He looked up at Rain. "The younger generation is truly a blessing. Tell me—were any others bearing cubs at the time?"

"One or two, I think," said Peony. "The only one I knew for certain was a panda whose territory bordered mine. She disappeared. I found the body of her mate, washed up on the shore."

"But she could still be out there," said Sunset thoughtfully. "And her cub, or cubs. Wouldn't it be wonderful if we could find her? If we could find all our missing family?"

The pandas all nodded solemnly at this. Rain did too, but she felt a prickle of discomfort between her shoulders as she did so. Obviously, she wanted her mother's friend and her cub to be alive, but was it really a good idea to make the Prosper-hill pandas think that all their missing friends could be out there somewhere? And what about the ones who knew their loved ones would never come home? What about Pebble?

The bamboo pile was just a scattering of dry sticks now, and Rain would have liked to climb down from her tree and find a comfortable place for a nap before the Feast of Moon Climb, but she sensed that the other pandas were still waiting for something, so she didn't move.

"Speaker," said Squall. "Can you still speak to the Dragon? Does it have any guidance for us?"

"Please," Horizon added, and several of the other pandas raised their voices in agreement. "Please, do you have a proph-ecy to share?"

Sunset sat back, and his eyes slowly closed. Rain leaned forward so far her paw slipped and she almost tumbled out of the tree before she caught herself. Was it really true? Was she about to see what a Dragon Speaker receiving a vision really looked like?

Eyes still shut, Sunset placed his forepaws down in front of him and dug his claws into the earth. He went very still, barely even breathing, as if he had been carved from stone. The pandas around him were almost as still as he was, though a few of them chewed their claws or scratched their bellies in anticipation.

Rain kept her gaze fixed on the old panda's face. When his eyes snapped open, it was so sudden it made her jump. Was she imagining it, or did they glint more brightly than they should have? They were certainly wide and full of something like amazement.

Sunset lifted his left front paw, and there was something held in it that glinted like the light in his eyes. It was a tiny, perfectly round, blue stone.

Mist let out a gasp. "The Seeing Stone," she whispered. "Through everything . . . you still have it!"

Rain cast a confused glance down at Peony, who reared up against the trunk of the tree to say quietly, "The Dragon Speakers have always carried the Seeing Stone. It's very old, and very powerful—it came from the cave where the Great Dragon lives!"

*Where is that cave?* Rain wondered. But before she could ask Peony, Sunset spoke, still holding up the blue orb.

"The Seeing Stone has told me the will of the Great Dragon," he said. Then he smiled, pure joy creasing the fur around his eyes. "The Great Dragon is pleased. You are already on the right path. When all the pandas are reunited, we will cross the waters together."

Several of the pandas gasped, and Squall sat back on his haunches with such force he almost toppled over backward.

"Did you hear that?" Cypress murmured to Horizon. "The Dragon wants us to be reunited. Some of the missing *must* still be out there!"

"If Citrus is alive, we'll find her," Horizon replied to her mate, nuzzling her nose against his cheek.

"The Great Dragon speaks once more!" Mist proclaimed, standing up on slightly wobbly legs. "Thank you, Dragon Speaker."

Rain sat on a tree branch that stretched out over the water, watching the moon glinting on the gold-speckled backs of the carp in the stream. She focused, waiting for just the right moment; then she thrust a paw down into the water and scooped out a wriggling fish. She held it up for a second in triumph, then let it slip from her grasp and splash back into the water again.

"You're safe, this time," she said to the dark water. "I'm not hungry enough to eat a fish today. But I could if I wanted to."

"Yuck," said Pebble's voice behind her. She turned to look at him as he stepped out from the shadow of the trees into the moonlight.

"Fish is okay," Rain said. "It's not bamboo, but I like how it tastes of the river."

Pebble walked to the edge of the water. The white parts of his fur almost seemed to glow as he looked down at the rippling reflections and then up at the starlit sky.

"Isn't it amazing?" he said.

Rain hesitated. She guessed he wasn't talking about the taste of fish.

"He's so *wise*," Pebble went on. "And did you see that scar? He must have been so brave, to escape those leopards. And he really *understands*, you know? I mean, his brother . . ." He trailed off, and Rain gave him a sympathetic look, though she found that her thoughts were a little bit less straightforward.

*Lots of us lost family. He's not the only one.* It was the first thing that leaped to her mind to say, but she knew it wouldn't exactly be kind to say it. *It must be nice for Pebble to feel like someone important shares his sadness.*

She looked out over the river. The far bank was invisible now, shrouded in darkness.

"Why do you think the Dragon wants us to cross over?" she wondered aloud.

"Hmm?" Pebble said, as if she'd interrupted his stream of thought.

"Well, Sunset said that the Dragon told him that when we're reunited, we'll cross the waters together, right? But the forest on the other side doesn't seem particularly great. I mean, I'd like to be able to swim across, but . . . what do you think the *point* is? And *how*? Will we all form a big panda chain across the river? What about the cubs? And Mist, and Squall? Surely he doesn't mean they'll *actually* cross over, does he?"

Pebble shook his head. "You take things too literally. He's the Dragon Speaker; he knows what he's talking about."

"I don't doubt it," said Rain, although deep down, a small, rebellious part of her did. "I'm just saying *I* don't know what he's—"

She broke off. She thought she'd heard voices coming from just around the riverbend. Pebble gave her a strange look, but Rain kept silent until she heard it again. . . .

". . . as I asked?"

Was that Sunset's voice?

"Oh yes, we found it all right."

The reply also sounded familiar, though Rain couldn't put her paw on where she'd heard it before. It didn't sound like any of the pandas—nor did the chorus of quiet hooting in agreement that followed.

Rain climbed along the tree branch and down onto the shore. With Pebble in tow, still slightly bemused, she snuck through the undergrowth and up and over a rock until she was looking down at a clearing where Sunset the Dragon Speaker was standing, looking up at the branches above him. For a moment Rain couldn't see who he was speaking to. Then she crouched back, pressing her belly to the rock, as she realized that the trees were full of golden monkeys. In the darkness their bright fur almost blended in with the golden leaves of the gingko tree, but there must have been at least ten of them, maybe more, all gathered and looking down at Sunset.

"Good work, Brawnshanks," Sunset said. "Give it to me."

One of the monkeys half climbed, half fell out of the tree,

catching himself on a low branch with his tail and presenting an armful of bamboo to Sunset with a flourish. Rain squinted in the dim light and saw that the leaves of the bamboo were covered in stripes of darker and paler green, and each growth section of the cane also seemed to be a different shade.

The monkey Brawnshanks cocked his head, and Rain saw that this was the same big monkey with the torn ear that she had argued with earlier that day.

But then he had been aggressive and bitter. He'd mocked the very idea that there would be a Dragon Speaker again, or that anyone would listen to the pandas. And now he was fetching bamboo for the Speaker, no more than two feasts after he had returned to the Prosperhill?

"I'll need more soon," said Sunset.

"Don't you worry about that," Brawnshanks said with a wink. "We'll keep you well supplied. Congrats again, Dragon Speaker."

With that, the monkey swung up into the trees, and the whole troop whooped again and scampered away, vanishing into the upper canopy.

Sunset gripped the strange striped bamboo carefully in his jaws, but he didn't chomp down on it as Rain thought he might. Instead he carried it away into the shadows under the trees, and was gone.

"What is he up to?" Rain wondered aloud.

"'Up to'?" Pebble frowned. "I think pretending to be a Dragon Speaker has messed with your head. He's just talking to the monkeys. That's good—that's what a Speaker ought to do."

"What about the bamboo?" Rain shot back.

"It looked tasty," Pebble said, rolling his big shoulders. "The monkeys must have brought it as a welcome-back gift."

"What, Brawnshanks?" She straightened up and adopted a haughty voice. "'Do this, or the Dragon will never speak to you again'? *That* Brawnshanks?"

"Look, he's the *Dragon Speaker*," Pebble said. He got to his paws and bumped Rain affectionately with one shoulder. "Don't be jealous. Are you really surprised the creatures of the Bamboo Kingdom are keen to get back in his good graces? If he needs that particular bamboo, he'll have a good reason, you'll see. Everything he does is for the good of the Bamboo Kingdom. That's what a Speaker is *for*."

"Yeah," said Rain, bumping him back. "Maybe he'll share this special bamboo at the Feast of Moon Climb."

But the words felt hollow in her mouth.

*Is it just me? Am I just jealous? Or is there really something here that's not quite right?*

# CHAPTER FIVE

THE MIST IN THE Northern Forest was so thick this morning that Leaf could barely see across the clearing to the other pandas. It curled between the trees, chilling the pandas' fur—and, worse, hiding the thin, weedy bamboo sprouts from them. It was a very paltry feast. Only Gale had managed to find a good-sized clump of new growth, and she had already shared her good luck with Hyacinth and Cane, whose search had come up practically empty.

"At the Feast of Gray Light, your humble pandas bow before you," intoned Crabapple, though his voice seemed thin and muffled in the fog. "Thank you for the gift of the bamboo, and the wisdom you bestow upon us."

Leaf tried to make her feast last as long as possible, but it was all gone in moments. There was a quiet in the Slenderwood clearing that had nothing to do with happy pandas munching on bamboo. Leaf guessed they were probably all wondering the same thing—if this mist didn't burn away soon, would they be able to find anything to eat at Golden Light? What about Sun Climb? Even once the mist lifted, if the growth was this bad, would there be bamboo to find at High Sun or Long Light?

"We cannot go on like this," said Aunt Plum in a firm voice, startling Leaf out of her worries. Several of the other pandas jumped too.

Grass shook her head. "We don't have a choice, do we? The Dragon has abandoned us. Unless we pick a direction and start walking, and hope that we come across a better place before we starve to death. . . ."

Cane made a soft whimpering noise, and Hyacinth pulled him close to her with a glare at Grass.

"We are wreathed in the Dragon's breath," said Plum. Her voice was quiet, but it seemed to command the attention of every panda in the clearing. "This mist is a sign. The Dragon wants us to do something. I . . . I don't know what it is yet. But I for one cannot go on like this. We must try to find out why there has been no new Dragon Speaker."

There was another long silence.

"How?" asked Juniper.

Plum sat back on her haunches and turned her face to the sky, as if she was hoping that the Dragon itself would finally intercede and tell her what to do. Leaf held her breath. What if it did? What if this time, just this once, there was a sign . . . ?

No sign came. Plum let out a sigh and returned her gaze to the rest of the pandas.

"I will go to the Dragon Mountain," she said. "I will make the journey to the cave. And if I don't receive a sign along the way, then I'll meet the Dragon face-to-face and ask what we can do to put things right."

Juniper blew out a huge breath through his nose, shaking his head.

"Oh, Plum," said Hyacinth. "No. It's too far; it's much too dangerous."

"No panda has made it to the cave—not since Sunset was chosen," said Crabapple.

"I think . . . perhaps you're right." Juniper got to his feet. "Someone must go. But I also think we may never see you again if you take this on, Plum. You must be certain."

"How could I be uncertain?" Plum looked around at the Slenderwood pandas, at the meager scraps of bamboo that had been their First Feast.

Leaf watched this exchange with a feeling like a hot spring bubbling up inside her, and now she couldn't hold it in anymore. She jumped to her paws.

"I'll go with you." She ran across the clearing to Aunt Plum. "It'll be safer with two. I'll go with you, and we'll find the Dragon together!"

Plum's eyes shone as she looked at Leaf. "Oh, my sweet Leaf. No," she said.

"What? Why not?" Leaf sat back on her haunches with a

soft thump. "You can't go alone—what if you don't come back to us?"

"That's exactly why I can't take you with me," Plum said. "I promised Orchid I wouldn't let anything happen to you. I couldn't risk your life like this. I know the pain of losing a cub," she added. "My own Cloud died just before Orchid left you with me. I nursed you, and I love you as much as I loved Cloud. I couldn't bear it if you were hurt, not for Orchid's sake or my own."

"I'd be fine," Leaf said, but weakly, knowing that it wasn't much of an argument in the face of Plum's grief. "I can climb. I can . . . I can take care of you."

"I love that you want to. But I can do this," Plum said, and leaned forward to lick Leaf between the eyes. Then she turned to the other pandas and set her paws firmly in the thin grass. "I will set off before Sun Climb."

Leaf ran down the forest slope, the bamboo she'd gathered held tightly but carefully in her jaws. The sun was rising and the mist was less now, though patches of it still lingered in the bottoms of the valleys and between the high rocks.

*I can't have missed her,* she thought. *She wouldn't have left, would she?*

Her heart juddered with relief as she skidded to a halt at the bottom of the slope and saw Plum, surrounded by the other Slenderwood pandas, saying goodbye to them one by one with a bump of the nose or a gentle pat on the shoulder. She rolled over and spread her arms playfully when she came to little Cane, and he roared in his small voice and jumped onto her belly. Plum gently moved him off and stood up.

Leaf paused just outside the group to steady herself. She couldn't imagine life without her aunt Plum. But she was right—someone had to find some answers, or none of them would survive much longer.

She trotted into the circle, and Plum turned to look at her.

"I brought you these for the journey," Leaf said, dropping the bamboo at her feet.

"Oh, Leaf." Plum gently bumped foreheads with her. "Your mother would be very proud of you. Now, don't forget—always say the blessing, even if the feast is a single leaf. Remember to groom behind your ears, especially after you've been climbing. Listen to your elders. Don't let those red pandas lead you anywhere you can't get back from."

"I'll remember," said Leaf.

"I'll see you very soon. Take care of them all for me," Plum added. Leaf drew herself up as tall as she could, and watched as Plum took the bamboo and turned to start on her long journey. The rest of the Slenderwood pandas called out their good wishes to Plum and then began to disperse, but Leaf sat still until her aunt had completely vanished over the rocks and between the sparse trees.

Her heart felt heavy, despite Plum's reassurances. But for now, there was nothing she could do.

She needed a distraction, she decided. She started walking toward the river. She would climb one of her favorite trees by the shore and see if she could see any movement on the far bank.

As she was walking, she heard a rustle in the undergrowth, and then a voice.

"Leaf! Hey Leaf! Wait for me!"

It was Dasher. Leaf stopped to let her small friend catch up. It didn't take long—somehow the red pandas always seemed to move faster on their little legs than a panda four times their size.

"I heard about Plum," Dasher said, sitting up on his haunches when he'd reached Leaf's side. "Wow. She's so brave."

Leaf nodded, and her heart felt a tiny bit lighter. "She is."

Dasher grinned, then put out his black paws and rested them on Leaf's chest. "She's going to be okay," he said. Leaf nodded again, but couldn't bring herself to reply. "Hey, hey, Leaf," Dasher went on, getting back down and bounding across the path in front of her. "I've got something to show you. Down by the river. You're going to want to see this!"

And with that he scampered off, running vertically up trees and over rocks, pausing every few seconds in his dash to look back and check she was following him. Leaf smiled and hurried after him. This was a pretty obvious ploy to distract her, but to be fair to Dasher, it was working. She was lucky to have a best friend like him.

Dasher led her down to the shore, to the place where instead of jutting rocks or tangled trees sticking up out of the river, there was an open, pebbled beach that sloped gently into the water. There were a handful of red pandas there already— Leaf recognized Jumper, as well as some of the older pandas whose names she didn't know, and Splasher Swimming Deep. Splasher was sitting on a rock in the shallows, her tail lashing back and forth as she stared into the water.

"They're still looking for a way to cross?" Leaf asked Dasher. "Even after what happened to Diver?"

"Especially," said Dasher, and lowered his voice as he added, "Splasher wants to do it in his name. Anyway, we don't give up on things. If the Great Dragon can't help us, we'll help ourselves. That's the red-panda way," he said, blinking proudly. "And today might be the day! Look!"

He scampered to the edge of the water and pointed with one of his small black front paws. Leaf looked, and her heart suddenly felt as light as air. A huge old bamboo trunk, nearly as wide around as Dasher's whole body, had fallen from the shore and was now sticking out over the fast-flowing center of the river.

"It doesn't go all the way to the other side," Dasher said.

"But it would give us a head start, take us across the worst of the current. We could make it!" Leaf was already walking toward the rocks where the base of the bamboo was, its roots still firmly embedded in the earth. Dasher scampered after her, and Splasher joined them, running up onto the rocks and looking along the length of the tree.

Leaf's belly fluttered, like branches tossed in the wind. *Can I really do this?* She leaned forward, tentatively placing one paw at a time on the bamboo. The thick stem creaked a little, but it didn't move.

"I'm going," Leaf said. "If I can get across, if I can find my mother . . . I have to try."

"I'm coming with you," Dasher said. He turned to Chomper. She gave him a solemn nod.

"I'll tell the Climbing Fars where you are," she said. "Good luck."

Dasher raised his tail in a kind of salute, and got on to the trunk behind Leaf.

Leaf looked out over the rushing water and took a few slow, calming breaths.

*Remember you're a panda,* she thought. *Go steady, be strong. You'll make it.*

She squared her shoulders and began to walk out over the river.

The bamboo creaked and swayed a little with each step, but it seemed to be holding firm. She told herself it was just like climbing, but in a different direction—paw over paw, reaching for claw holds in the smooth woody surface, and not looking down.

"Still with me?" she called back to Dasher, without turning around—the movement of doing so could be enough to throw her balance off.

"Yep, yep, still here," said Dasher.

The trunk started out suspended about two bear-lengths above the water, and the weight of the two friends bent it down a little, but Leaf knew that bamboo this old and thick could take a huge amount of pressure. It held them both up above the water until they were over the middle of the wide river, and a little bit farther. Then it began to thin, and Leaf gripped the sides with her claws as it bent down toward the cold water.

"Not much farther," she said. "Then we're going to have to swim for it."

The bank opposite seemed so close now, she could almost feel her paws on the soft, mossy earth. It would be a tough swim, but she could make it, and once she was there, surely it wouldn't be hard to find Orchid and her sibling. . . .

Then the bamboo beneath Leaf's paws jolted suddenly downward. A *c-r-r-a-a-ck!* echoed from the cliffs on either side of the river. Leaf crouched and dug her claws into the thick bamboo as it dipped and bounced under her.

"Leaf!" Dasher gasped. "It's—"

The water came up to meet them, and Dasher's words were cut off as he, Leaf, and the whole bamboo trunk plunged into the river. Water splashed up Leaf's nose and soaked her to the skin in an instant, waves crashed against her flank, and the bamboo rolled and bobbed in the water, but she wrapped herself around it and held on with all her might. At last her head broke the surface long enough for her to let out a roar of fear.

"Dasher!" Leaf glanced back over her shoulder, terrified that she would see her best friend's small body being dragged under by the current. But Dasher had managed to cling on to the bamboo too, though his fluffy red fur and striped tail were waterlogged. Behind him, the bamboo had come free of the earth completely—she could see cracks in the trunk and the straggling ends of roots—and now Leaf realized that the whole thing was floating downriver, driven along by the currents. The beach, Splasher, the whole Slenderwood, all of it was receding quickly into the distance behind them.

"We've got to get off this thing!" Dasher squeaked.

Leaf tried to look at the river in front of them, and spluttered as another wave rolled over her head.

*By the Nine Feasts,* she thought desperately, *I would have been safer going with Plum to the mountain! I promised her I'd stay safe, and now...*

But there was no time to chide herself. Somewhere up ahead, she knew, there were sharp rocks that split the river into churning rapids. If they couldn't stop before they reached them . . .

"Climb back!" she yelled to Dasher. "Get back to the thicker end!"

Dasher turned, his nimble paws clutching the trunk, and started unsteadily running back. To follow him, Leaf had to let herself slide into the river with her back paws, and then claw her way along, pointing her nose in the air to try to keep it above water.

*If we can get closer to the northern bank, maybe we can swim for it,* she thought. *We have to try!*

"Over here! Panda! Here!" cried a voice above her. She looked up, trying to blink the wet fur from her eyes. Two small shapes were bounding from branch to branch in the trees along the northern shore. One of them sprang from a tree, and the fur between its arms and legs splayed out, letting it glide through the air to the trunk.

Flying squirrels!

"Root coming!" one of the squirrels squeaked urgently. "Get it! Grab it!"

Leaf peered over the bamboo trunk and saw it. A bend in the river where rocks and the roots of trees stuck out in a trailing tangle.

"Dasher, jump for it!" she roared. "Go!"

Dasher bunched his muscles, ran along the bamboo trunk, and leaped, flying through the air almost as if he could glide like the squirrels. His front paws connected with the root, and he pushed down, rolling over through the air to land in a tangle on the shore.

*It's now or never,* Leaf thought. She pushed off from the bamboo, trying to propel herself as close to the roots as she could. She knew at once she was going to fall short. The water was dragging her down. So she took a deep breath and dived, pushing underneath the water. She fought to open her eyes, and saw the roots ahead as they stretched down under the water. With paw-strokes that seemed to take all her strength, she battled against the current to reach them. Her chest became tight and panic gripped her, but then her claws found purchase on the underwater roots and she began to climb.

Her nose broke the surface, and she almost head-butted Dasher, whose concerned face was peering over the edge of the tangled roots. He yelped and scampered backward.

"Leaf! You're alive! You made it!" He grabbed at Leaf's front leg with his paws as she pulled herself up and over onto solid ground, and Leaf appreciated the attempt to help, even though he was far too small to hold on to her. "We saw you go underwater. I thought you'd drowned!"

"I made it," Leaf echoed, gasping and coughing up river water.

She sank to her belly against the trunk of the tree that had saved them and tried to catch her breath.

"What a pair of idiots," said a voice above her, and she looked up to see the flying squirrels, clinging upside down to the trunk of the tree.

"Did you really think you could make it to the other side?" the other squirrel said.

"It's too far," the first one shook its head at Leaf. "Especially for a panda. No offense, cub. But if we can't even glide across, how's a big old bear like you going to make it?"

"Get used to living in the Northern Forest, you two," said the second squirrel as it started to climb back up the tree. "Because you're never going to leave it."

# CHAPTER SIX

The Endless Maw.

Ghost trod the snow at his paws into a packed shelf as he looked down into the yawning depths of the crevasse. He had no words for how big it was—he could guess that twenty leopards standing nose to tail would barely stretch across the top, but when it came to the fall . . . he couldn't even guess. The crack in the mountain was so deep that even the snow couldn't seem to reach the bottom. Great sheets of it blew in and piled up in drifts against the jagged walls, but in the depths all Ghost could see was blackness.

"Woooooow," breathed Shiver, and stepped closer to Ghost. "We . . . we really have to jump that?"

"When we're ready," said Frost faintly.

"Look," said Snowstorm, her voice a little quivery. "There's the column."

Ghost didn't see it at first. All he could see was the deep, deep drop below him. But then his swimming vision finally focused on a wide column of rock that stood up in the middle of the crevasse.

"So it's only half as far as it looks, really," Snowstorm went on, drawing herself up tall and stiffening her tail.

Frost shook himself, and Ghost startled and dug his claws into the snow. He felt as if the sudden movement could make him slip and fall into the blackness, even though he was a leopard-length away from the edge.

"It's too far." Shiver shook her head. "I'll never make it."

"None of us are old enough yet," Frost said, giving her a reassuring lick on the side of her face. "You'll be ready one day."

Ghost felt the fur on his back prickle and a warm flush of embarrassment run down his spine, despite the frozen winds. The air felt heavy with the words none of his siblings were saying.

Shiver probably would be ready one day. But Ghost . . .

"Come on, let's practice!" Snowstorm said, and Ghost's heart sank even further as she turned and trotted toward the maze of rocks that stuck up from the snowdrifts a little way away. They were a variety of heights and distances apart—perfect for cubs to practice their leaping, knowing there was soft snow waiting to catch them when they fell. Winter said that as long as there had been leopards on the White Spine, which was always, they had jumped the Endless Maw to prove themselves, and had practiced on the Training Rocks.

*Don't talk yourself down,* he told himself, trying to hear his mother's voice in his head. *You can get better. That's what practicing is for.*

Shiver climbed up onto one of the lower rocks and wiggled her tail as she crouched, assessing the distance to the next one.

"You can do it!" Frost called out encouragingly. Shiver took a deep breath and leaped, soared through the air, and landed steadily on the rock about a leopard-length away.

"Yeah!" said Snowstorm. "There you go! Now try to get to the next one. Don't forget to use your tail for balance."

Frost peeled away and headed for one of the other rocks, while Snowstorm stayed to cheer Shiver on a little more. Ghost watched as Frost focused on a rock almost as far from him as the column in the middle of the Maw was from the edge. He held his breath as his brother tensed and sprang. Could he really do it? Was Frost ready?

For a moment he thought he would make it, but Frost fell short and landed face-first in the snow, sending a big white cloud puffing out all around him. Ghost suppressed the urge to laugh as Frost scrambled out of the bank, shook himself, and then sat down and licked his paws as if he'd meant to do that all along.

"Come on, Ghost!" Shiver called. She was sitting proudly on the next rock along, trembling as she caught her breath, but her eyes bright at having made it across the small jumps. Snowstorm had moved away to practice on some of the higher rocks—she chose one with a difficult jump, but nowhere near as far as Frost's, and Ghost saw her soar across the gap. She landed awkwardly but stuck out her tail and steadied herself.

Ghost glanced back at his own tail, or tried to. His lit-termates all had long, wide, fluffy tails that were perfect for helping with balance—Shiver's was as long as her whole body. But his tail was still so short and stumpy he couldn't even see it properly unless he lay on his side and twisted himself into a circle.

He climbed up onto a rock and eyed the distance between it and the next. It wasn't very far. He was much bigger than Shiver. He had longer legs, and he was stronger. There was no reason he couldn't do this.

He fixed his gaze on the rock ahead of him, crouched back, tensed his muscles, and leaped with all his might.

For a moment, he felt like he was flying.

Then he crashed into the snow, his front claws catching painfully on the very edge of the rock, but the rest of him fall-ing a long way short.

The sound of two cackling voices made him wince. He rolled over and sat up, blowing the snow from his muzzle and keeping his eyes closed. Of *course* those two were here to see that. Perhaps if he kept his eyes shut and didn't move, the snow would eventually cover him and he would never have to face the cubs Born of Icebound, or jump the Endless Maw.

"Shut up!" he heard Snowstorm snap. He opened one eye and saw her jumping down from a rock.

"Did you see that?" Brisk purred. "Did you see that freak's excuse for a *jump*?"

Sleet flopped down and rolled over in the snow, still

laughing. "I can't believe that thing thinks he belongs here!"

"He *does* belong," Frost snarled, leaping down to join Snowstorm as Ghost came forward to stand shoulder-to-shoulder with his littermates.

"Oooh, I'm scared," sneered Sleet. "The freak can't jump, can't hunt. I bet he can't even run." He got to his paws and squared off with Ghost. "Can you run, freak?"

"Just ignore him," Frost muttered.

But Ghost was tired of being silent.

"I can," he said.

"You want to prove it?" Sleet's tail twitched with amusement. "How about a race?"

"Ghost . . . ," Snowstorm warned, but Ghost cut in before she could finish warning him not to take the bait.

"Fine by me."

"Ooooh," Brisk cooed. "How about from that rock to that pine tree?"

Ghost didn't reply. He just walked calmly over to the rock and sat down, waiting for Sleet.

"You can do it, Ghost," Shiver said, as Sleet strutted through the snow and sat beside him.

*Maybe I can,* Ghost thought. The tree wasn't so far away, and he could be fast, when he put his mind to it.

"Ready . . . go!" yelled Brisk.

Ghost sprang forward. His paws thumped down on the packed snow in a thundering rhythm, his strong legs carrying him faster and faster. He dared to split his attention for a second and saw that Sleet was behind him, paws scrabbling.

Ghost's heart soared and he put on another burst of speed.

But they were barely halfway to the tree when Ghost began to slow. No matter how hard he pushed, his lungs were starting to burn and his legs just wouldn't keep up the pace. Sleet drew level and then overtook, kicking a shower of snow into Ghost's face as he sprinted past.

"What's the matter?" the cub called back. Ghost tried to ignore him and kept on running, though now every step felt as if the snow were sticking him to the ground. Sleet laughed again—how did he have the breath left to laugh?—and swerved from the course, running in a circle around Ghost, once, twice, three times before heading at the tree at a casual trot. Ghost put his head down. He might have lost, but he wouldn't stop. He wouldn't let them see how tired he was. He wouldn't . . .

Something sharp struck his paw, and he tripped. The world lurched around him, as if it had risen up to throw him onto his face. He collapsed and rolled to a stop against a snowdrift, which crumbled and cascaded down to cover him from ears to tail.

"Ghost!"

Before he could stand up by himself, there was a swift scampering of paws on snow and his littermates were with him, Frost digging him out from the drift and Snowstorm sniffing anxiously at him.

"Are you hurt?"

"No," Ghost rasped, still so out of breath that sparkling lights flashed in front of his eyes for a moment as he stood up and shook off the wet snow. "I'm fine."

"Can't jump, can't run, can't even stand on his own paws!" Brisk yowled in a singsong voice, pouncing near Ghost and then leaping away again.

"What a freak! Can't run, can't jump!" Sleet sat just out of reach, washing his face with one paw.

Ghost's front left paw still ached where he'd hit it on the hidden rock, but he didn't let it show as he walked up to Sleet and bared his teeth.

"Want me to show you what I *can* do?" he roared.

Brisk stopped hopping back and forth and came to Sleet's side. He still spoke with a sneer, but Ghost could tell that he was worried. "We're not on your territory now. The Maw is for *all* leopards. We have every right to be here."

"And we have every right to wipe that smug look off your whiskers," growled Snowstorm.

"I bet he'd like that," said Brisk. "His littermates leaping to his defense yet again."

"Or we could let Ghost break you in half with one bite," said Shiver. "He could do that, you know. Ghost's got a bite that can break *rocks*."

Before Brisk or Sleet could reply, there was a roar as loud as a rumble of thunder. All six leopard cubs jumped at the sound and cringed back as, pounding over the snowfield, came a fully grown adult leopard, her teeth bared and her tail lashing angrily behind her.

"Mother!" Sleet yelped, running to the leopard and putting her between him and the cubs Born of Winter.

"They were going to let the white freak eat us!" Brisk yowled.

"Get away from my cubs!" Icebound snarled, pacing back and forth, her pale eyes fixed on Ghost. Ghost was already almost as big as her, but she was still an imposing figure, her teeth sharp, her shoulders tensed to spring, and her huge white paws digging deep grooves in the snow as she padded back and forth.

Snowstorm and Frost backed off, and Frost nudged Ghost and Shiver to do the same. Icebound watched them like they were prey, advancing even as they retreated.

"Maybe I should send you back to your softhearted mother with a scar or two," she growled, cocking her head at Ghost. "Maybe then she'd realize that you don't belong here. Keeping the runt is bad enough, but the white freak . . . I told her you'd be nothing but trouble. She should have *eaten* you when she had the chance. Now someone needs to drive you away from the White Spine, for good—"

"Ghost isn't going anywhere!" The defiant snarl came from behind Ghost's shoulder.

He spun around, kicking up snow, and saw Winter. She was standing on a tall snowbank, her teeth bared at Icebound, her tail vibrating with anger. She crouched and leaped, right over the heads of her cubs, and landed in the snow in front of Icebound, kicking up a flurry that flew right into the other leopard's face. Icebound roared and shook her head to clear the snow from her eyes as Winter stalked closer.

"He's my cub, and this is his home," she snarled. "They're all my cubs, and they're worth ten of your little bullies."

"Come here and say that!" Icebound spat, still swiping at her whiskers.

"Gladly!" Winter said, and pounced. Icebound was ready for her, but only just. They locked into a grapple, Winter's huge paws slamming into the side of Icebound's head and flank, rolling her over in the snow.

"Get her, Mother!" Sleet yowled, though he and Brisk had both scampered back to a safe distance.

Ghost couldn't bring himself to speak, but he watched in intense silence as Winter and Icebound twisted, broke away from each other, circled, and sprang again. Icebound got a hard smack in on the side of Winter's face, but then Winter threw her head back, roared, and sank her fangs into Icebound's shoulder.

Ghost's breath caught. He had seen his mother hunt, of course, but he'd never seen her fight another leopard before.

Icebound pushed her away and they sprang apart. Winter crouched, ready to pounce, but held back, waiting to see what the wounded leopard would do. Icebound licked at the wound and then spat red into the snow at her feet.

"You could kill me," she said. "My cubs would survive without my help." Ghost glanced behind her and saw Brisk and Sleet draw closer together and look at each other in dismay.

*They don't look like* they *think so,* Ghost thought.

"*But . . .* yours need your protection, that much is clear," Icebound went on, and stepped back, her posture relaxing.

Winter remained tense for a little longer, waiting for Icebound to retreat even farther. Then she nodded once and pulled herself up straight. She didn't say anything more as Icebound turned her back and walked away, sweeping Brisk and Sleet along in her wake. Winter stayed perfectly still until they had vanished over a snowdrift.

A high-pitched rumble from just behind Ghost's shoulder made him look around. It was Shiver, growling.

"What a coward! She made it sound like she *chose* to let you win." She padded up to their mother and looked up at her, a questioning frown on her face. "Why didn't you say something?"

Winter turned to look at her, and the stern expression melted into a fond smile. She licked Shiver hard between the eyes.

"Because we're better than them," she said. "Come on. Let's go home."

Ghost's paw didn't hurt too much while they were still walking through deep snow, but as they descended the mountain toward Winter's cave, it began to sting more and more. The cave was tucked in a shady, sheltered valley, where the snow hadn't fallen this season, and the ground was made up of layered rocks that overlapped each other with thin, pale grass growing in little clumps between them. Ghost usually found the rocks easier to walk on than snow, but right now each step on the hard ground felt like a jab against his pads, and by the time they got back to the cave, he was limping badly.

"Let's get you inside," Winter said gently. "And I'll have a look at that for you."

The inside of the cave was warm and soft, padded with many seasons of Winter's shed fur. The four cubs all flopped down in the comfortable nest, Snowstorm and Frost curling around Shiver, grooming each other to clear the last of the snow from their fur.

Ghost sat down and raised his front paw, and Winter began to gently lick at the cut on his pad.

"Me next," said Frost, purring.

"You'll each get a turn," Winter promised, blinking happily.

The cubs could all groom themselves, but it was so nice when their mother washed them. Ghost sighed happily, even though his pad still stung and one of his claws felt wobbly and sore. Part of him never wanted to leave the cave. He wanted to be a good leopard and hunt for himself, but in that moment, even if he could make the leap over the Maw, he thought it would be just as good to stay with Winter.

"Be careful of your pad for a few days," Winter said. "You've cracked a claw. And you must take no notice of Icebound," she added softly. "She's jealous of our territory, and the fact that there are four of you to carry my name into the world and she only has two cubs. She's made them into bullies because she's afraid of losing her territory once they leave her."

Ghost curled up, resting his chin against Winter's flank.

"I know," he said. "I just wish they'd leave me alone. I *know* I'm a freak," he went on, in a very small voice. "They don't need to keep reminding me."

"You're special," Winter said firmly. "You and Shiver are both very special. The Snow Cat brought you to me. It was a clear night. . . ."

She curled her tail around him and licked his ears. Ghost closed his eyes. He liked to listen to this story with them shut, so he could imagine it more clearly.

"The stars were bright, and the moon was a perfect circle. It lit up the White Spine Mountains, so strong that it was like daylight. You could look down over the cliff and see the trees in the forest waving in the breeze. I could hear birds singing, thinking it was the morning. Everything was very still. It was a perfect night for the Snow Cat to bring me my perfect cubs. And when you were born, a beam of moonlight shone down and turned your fur pure white. It made you glow, as if your light were coming from within. I knew right then that you were going to be special."

Shiver got up from her position between her siblings and walked outside the cave. Ghost's heart felt tight for a moment. Was she upset that Winter was telling this story? After all, she had been born different too.

But then she came back inside and padded up to Ghost. She licked him on his nose, and then reared up and patted his fur with her paws, leaving spots of mud, just like the spots on her own back.

"You're special," she said. "But you're still my brother. We know you're one of us, even if the idiots born of Icebound don't."

Ghost smiled and blew a huff of air in Shiver's face, and she giggled, like she always did.

But as he settled back against Winter's flank, he couldn't help wishing that his new spots weren't just pretend.

*They won't help me run or jump or hunt like a normal leopard,* he thought. *And Brisk and Sleet won't be fooled.*

*They'll always see me as a freak.*

*I am a freak.*

# CHAPTER SEVEN

THE PROSPERHILL PANDAS LAZED in the feast clearing, the soft light of Sun Climb bathing them and a cool breeze blowing through the Southern Forest. Rain stuffed a big pawful of bamboo leaves into her mouth and chewed thoughtfully. She had to admit that having the Dragon Speaker in their midst had brought a kind of peace to the Prosperhill. There was much less bickering. Even the older, grumpier pandas seemed to be on their best behavior with the Speaker around.

*But what about the monkeys? And the striped bamboo?*

Rain chomped the end of a bamboo cane as she considered what she'd heard the day before Moon Climb.

Sunset hadn't brought the special bamboo to the feast. And there was nothing wrong with that. There was no rule that said pandas couldn't eat between feasts, or save particularly tasty bamboo to eat later on. They did that all the time.

*Why don't I feel reassured by that thought?*

Suddenly, Sunset threw his bamboo shoots aside with a decisiveness that was almost a flourish.

All around the clearing, pandas froze in surprise, jaws full of bamboo, canes halfway to their mouths. The sprout that Blossom had been about to eat fell from her paws and bounced down from her rock.

"I just can't do it," Sunset sighed. "I can't eat another mouthful."

The pandas gasped as one. The Feast of Sun Climb had only just begun—for a grown panda to not want their feast was practically unheard of. Rain shifted her weight in the crook of her tree and peered down at Sunset. Was he ill?

"Not while there are so many of our brothers and sisters out there, missing, driven from their homes by the flood, just as I was."

The pandas relaxed a little, but only a little. They looked thoughtful, rather than dismayed.

"They need us, my friends. If even one panda is wandering in the wild, without knowing that their family is still alive . . ."

Rain saw Cypress and Pebble and some of the others nodding along, and took a thoughtful chew on her bamboo cane.

*"Rain!"* a voice hissed.

Rain looked down to see Peony glaring up at her from her spot against the trunk of the tree.

"What?" Rain whispered back.

"Don't eat while the Speaker is talking!" her mother shot back.

Rain slowly lowered the bamboo, embarrassed, but a little

perplexed and annoyed too. She'd never been told not to eat while a panda was talking before, but her mother was looking at her as if it were common sense.

"I was so lost," Sunset was saying. "And if there's even one panda out there who feels as I did, and we can bring them to live here in safety and happiness, then we must—we *will*—do so. We can wait no longer. As soon as this feast is concluded, we will begin our search."

There were roars of support and agreement as Sunset took up his bamboo again. The pandas fell back to eating, some of them clearly eager to get the feast over with so they could start searching. Pebble swallowed his bunch of leaves in two quick chomps, and then turned to Rain and gave her a huge hopeful grin. He climbed up the tree to sit on the branch next to hers.

"Rain, what if . . . ," he started. "What if Stone's still alive? What if we can find him, and Citrus, and all of them?"

Rain longed to be happy and excited with him. But what were the chances that Stone had lived, when Pebble had seen him dragged under the water and carried away?

"I need four volunteers to lead the search," Sunset announced, and a few pandas immediately stepped forward: Cypress, Blossom, Ginseng, and Lily. "Each of you will lead a few pandas away from here, each in a different direction. Seek any sign of other pandas, living or dead. Ask the creatures you meet. You will have to hold your own feasts while you're gone. If you find a panda, bring them back with you. If you don't, I'm trusting you to know when you need to turn back. Is that all clear?"

The four volunteer leaders nodded solemnly.

"And who will accompany these brave leaders?" Sunset called out.

There was a brief flurry of discussion, and Rain saw Horizon pat Fir gently on the head and turn to Sunset. "I will go with my mate," she said. "Dawn will take care of Fir while I'm away." She walked over to stand next to Cypress, who gave her a deeply grateful look.

"I'll go."

"I'll go." Granite and Bay had both spoken at once, and Sunset beckoned both of them forward.

"I'll go too," said Pebble.

Rain's gaze snapped around to him as he climbed down from the tree and stood beside the rest of the volunteers. He looked small compared to the full-grown pandas, but he held himself steadily and looked into Sunset's eyes.

"Pebble, isn't it?" Sunset said, and Pebble seemed to lose a little of his composure as the Dragon Speaker said his name.

"I'm going with him," Rain called out. She half clambered, half fell from the tree and trotted over to Pebble's side. "I'll go. With Pebble."

Pebble gave her an affectionate, grateful head-butt.

But Peony came hurrying over. "Rain! What are you thinking?" She turned to the Dragon Speaker. "I'm sorry, Sunset. They don't know what they're agreeing to. They're far too young. I know if Pebble's mother were still alive, she would say the same."

"But old enough to make brave choices," Sunset said gently.

"I commend you both, young ones. Don't trouble yourself, Peony; they will be quite safe."

"Well," Peony said, "just be careful. And stick with the older pandas. And make sure you eat enough. And . . ." As her mother spoke, Rain was aware of Sunset's keen gaze. It seemed to look right through her. Could he tell she had reservations about him? Could he tell that she was only volunteering to look after Pebble? She wanted to help him find his brother, but she wasn't exactly hopping for joy about this plan. . . .

If he could tell any of that, he didn't seem to mind. "Very well, then," he said. "Granite, you can go with Lily—you and Cypress and Horizon can split up and head into the mountains, as high as you can go. Bay, travel with Ginseng along the river toward the sunrise. And the two young heroes can go with Blossom toward the sunset."

*Oh.* Rain sighed. Of course she'd be assigned to Blossom. *We'd better find a stray panda soon. . . .*

She padded over and sat down beside Blossom, giving her a bright and cheery smile because she knew it would annoy her. Sure enough, Blossom huffed and looked away imperiously.

"My brave pandas. I believe that what you set out to do today is the will of the Great Dragon, and the only way to ensure the safety of all pandas everywhere. We will think of you all at every feast until you return with news. May the Great Dragon guide you!"

"I'm heading for that peak over there," Blossom snorted as they made their way to the edge of the Prosperhill. She pointed with her nose through a gap in the trees. Rain squinted up to see a tall, craggy hill that rose in the distance, its slopes thick with trees, beyond the bend in the river. "You two had better not slow me down."

"No way," said Pebble. "My brother might be out there somewhere. I won't stop for anything but the Nine Feasts!"

Blossom seemed pleased with this. Rain padded along silently behind them both. She kept looking up at the peak as it came in and out of view through gaps in the trees. It was far enough away that the mists surrounded its base and the trees looked blue and cold. And yet they could see it even from the Prosperhill.

*If there's a panda living there,* she thought, *why wouldn't they have made their way here already?*

*If they didn't want to come, why would we make them?*

*If there's no panda there, do we press on? How long for? Nine feasts? Eighteen? Forever? If we come back alone, will Sunset be angry with us?*

The longer they walked, alongside the river and up the sides of the hills, climbing over rocks and around trees, the more ifs seemed to crowd into Rain's head. At last they found a new clump of bamboo forest, and Blossom declared it was time for the Feast of High Sun. She claimed the closest bamboo stand for herself, and sent Rain and Pebble away to look for sprouts of their own.

As she and Pebble walked away from Blossom to look for bamboo, Rain found she couldn't keep her questions to herself any longer. She waited until she was certain the selfish older panda wouldn't hear her; then she nudged her best friend with one shoulder.

"Hey, Pebble," she said, trying to sound casual. "Does this mission seem . . . odd to you?"

"Odd? How?" Pebble asked, his jaws full of bamboo canes.

"Well . . . we all live on the Prosperhill together now. But it's only because of the flood, right? Because it's safe and there's plenty of bamboo and the land is still unstable in other places. Mother's always telling us that."

"Right."

"But the older pandas are always going on about how things were better before, when we had our own territories. If there are pandas out there, alive, this long after the flood, and they're surviving okay without us . . . aren't they just doing what pandas are supposed to do? Why would the Dragon Speaker want us to bring them here, where it's already crowded?"

To Rain's dismay, Pebble's expression drew into a dark frown. He dropped his bamboo canes.

"Listen, I know you don't get it," he snapped. "You wouldn't. You didn't lose anyone."

Rain bristled. "Hey. My father died. Remember? I know Mother doesn't like to talk about him much, and I know I was too young to remember what happened, but you can't tell me I didn't lose anyone!"

"Sorry." Pebble scratched at the ground with one paw, leaving deep grooves in the leaf mulch. "I didn't mean that. But that's all the more reason—if you thought maybe your father could be out there somewhere, wouldn't you want to find him? Stone could be alive. I know it's a slim chance; I'm not stupid.

But like you said, things are unstable out there. There are still storms and rockfalls and stuff going on. What if pandas *want* to come to join us, but they're trapped or scared?"

"I get that," Rain admitted. "I just . . . There's no evidence there *are* other pandas out there."

Pebble's dark look returned. "I can't believe you still think Sunset's up to something!" he huffed. "Just because *you're* always playing tricks to get out of your duties, that doesn't mean every panda's as selfish as you."

Rain's jaw dropped. "I am not selfish!"

"You are! And—and it's fine. You can live your life like that if you want, but don't pretend the Dragon Speaker is doing something wrong just so you can feel better about not being able to lie to the cubs anymore."

"That is *not* what this is—" Rain began, but then broke off. She stared at Pebble, her best friend, standing there in front of her telling her that she was a selfish liar. How dare he? She didn't need to defend herself to him. "Look, if you want to believe there's some Great Dragon behind everything and Sunset is perfect and nothing's weird about any of this, that's up to you. But I'm telling you, something here doesn't make sense."

"Then why are you here?" Pebble growled. "If you think it's so wrong to look for pandas who need our help, why did you come?"

*To look after you, you idiot,* Rain thought. But she was too upset with him to say it out loud.

"That's a good question," she snarled back. "I'm leaving.

You and Blossom can go on your fool's errand all by your-selves. Come and talk to me when you figure out that I'm right."

And with that she turned tail and stomped away through the bamboo canes, shoving them aside with her shoulders as she walked.

"Fine!" Pebble shouted after her. "And you can apologize to me when I come back with my brother!"

As she walked, Rain growled to herself in a low, persistent rumble. This was fine. It was better this way. If Pebble was going to be all sensitive about her questioning the Dragon Speaker, then they would never have made it to that peak without fighting. *Let him and Blossom get on with their mission, and when they return home . . .*

She stumbled to a halt and rested her forehead against a tree trunk.

When they got back—brother or not—she'd say sorry. She shouldn't have let that argument get out of control.

She walked on, heading downhill. She wasn't sure exactly where she was, but if she followed the slope she would reach the river, and she'd feel better when she was in the water. She always did.

As she walked, she stomped her paws in the soft moss, annoyed with herself, but more and more annoyed with Sun-set Deepwood. It was his fault, really, that this had happened. And she *wasn't* wrong: *something* was definitely strange about him. Maybe he meant well, and maybe it would be good to search the kingdom for pandas who needed help, but it still bothered her that she was the only one who seemed to be willing to ask the obvious questions. It itched under her claws, like there was a bug stuck between her paw pads. And there was still the business with Brawnshanks and the striped bamboo to account for. Sunset had said he would need more. *Why?*

Well, there was nothing stopping her from trying to find out.

She hurried down the slope until she came to a jutting rock and a gap between the trees, and saw the river glistening in the High Sun. She realized that she hadn't had her feast, and her stomach rumbled guiltily. But she could catch up later, and if the other pandas were busy eating right now, that would mean they couldn't run into her and ask what she was doing.

She took a moment to get her bearings, looking across the river at the opposite bank. Then she turned to her left and made her way along the slope, keeping the river close on one side. And, sure enough, as the High Sun was starting to shift into Long Light, she came out into a small clearing beside the water, surrounded by tall gingko trees, with a big rock shelf rising on one side where a panda could sneak up and look down into the clearing.

This was it. Sunset had met Brawnshanks and the other golden monkeys here.

Rain looked up into the trees first, suddenly wary. Was that the tail of a monkey hanging down from that branch? Had something moved between the leaves? But after a few moments of sharp attention, she concluded it was just some waving ivy. She was alone.

She stepped into the center of the clearing and began to

sniff around on the ground. If she was lucky, the monkeys or Sunset would have dropped a sprig of that striped bamboo, and she could get a closer look at it. She could scent pandas—faint old scents of Prosperhill pandas who'd wandered here before, and the much more recent, still-foreign scent of Sunset himself. And she could smell monkeys, too, the weird sharp stink of the fruit they liked to eat.

But there was no bamboo. She even climbed unsteadily up into one of the gingko trees to search the branches in case a stray leaf had been caught up there, but there was nothing.

She snorted to herself as she tumbled back down to the ground. She supposed she hadn't thought it would be easy to work out what Sunset was up to, but she'd hoped there would be *something*.

She rooted around near the shore until she found some bamboo, and took it to the edge of the river. There was a small waterfall just by the clearing, where the rocks stuck up out of the river in a pattern that made the water snake through them and then crash into a sheltered pool before rejoining the main stream. A fine mist sprayed up from the pool, and dancing patterns of light shone on the rocks all around when the sun was high.

Rain settled down on a flat rock beside the waterfall, holding the bamboo in her hands. She opened her mouth to start saying the blessing, but then stopped. What was she saying it *for*? If she really wasn't sure there was a Great Dragon, why would she thank it for the bamboo that she'd picked herself, or for the peace that she really wasn't feeling right now?

She remembered Sunset holding his bamboo aloft and declaiming the blessing, and that decided it for her. With a thrill of rebellion, she crunched into the bamboo, enjoying the stillness all around her, broken only by the gentle churning of the water in the pool. The spray settled on her fur, pleasantly cooling. She closed her eyes, enjoying the fresh green taste of the bamboo and the splash of the water.

As she listened, the splashing seemed to grow a little louder. And then a lot louder. She opened her eyes and stared at the waterfall. What was happening to it? The water didn't *look* like it was running faster, but the sound had become a roar, as if the whole river were crashing down a cliff side, and the spray suddenly felt *warm*. It couldn't just be the sun hitting her fur; it felt like the warmth was bubbling up from the pool itself.

*What is going on?*

Rain leaned over the edge of her rock to look closer, and then rolled back as a huge plume of hot mist billowed up into her face. It seemed to surround her for a moment, and then it moved in a way she'd never seen mist or steam move before, writhing into a long, thin shape that curled in the air in front of her, massive and almost solid-looking. At the end of the writhing column, it split into three, and the three ends turned at once toward Rain, and she suddenly saw what they were.

Reptilian heads, with tendrils of steam trailing from their chins and their ears, shimmering rainbows making scale patterns across their snouts, and large, swirling eyes. Three heads that opened their mouths and roared at Rain, showing off teeth made from pointed columns of scalding hot steam.

Rain let out a shriek and fell backward off her rock. She scrambled to her feet and back up onto the rock, but when she got there, the air was cool again and the cloud of steam was dispersing softly into the wind—just a cloud, with no sign of scales or teeth or a winding body.

There was no sign of a dragon.

Rain's paws trembled as she stepped forward and looked down at the pool. She turned to look around at the forest, but nothing seemed to have changed. And no mischievous creatures seemed to be lurking to make fun of her for falling for their trick, either.

Slowly, her fear and shock began to turn to anger. She planted her paws on the rock.

"What was that?" she demanded. "Show yourself if you're really there!"

There was no answer but the burbling of the tiny waterfall.

"I fell asleep," she muttered to herself. "That must be it. Sunset's nonsense got to me and I dreamed I saw a dragon." The longer she thought about it, the more she realized that that *must* be true. The pool suddenly turning hot, a three-headed dragon made of steam? There was no way that could have been real. She snorted contemptuously and turned her back on the river to finish eating her bamboo. Sunset had clearly gotten into her head, but she was going to figure out what was going on with him, if it was the last thing she did.

# CHAPTER EIGHT

LEAF COVERED HER EYES with her paws. "Up the hill or around the bend, I will find you in the end!" she sang. "One. Two. Three . . ."

She heard the sounds of giggling and scampering paws, and she was sorely tempted to peek between her claws and see where her friends were hiding themselves. But however much fun it was to win the finding game, it was always more fun to win it fairly. She counted until she couldn't hear the sounds anymore, then counted ten more; then she opened her eyes.

The Northern Forest was quiet. Leaf didn't get up at once, but looked and listened for any movement. She knew that Roller Digging Deep liked to hide close to the finder so he could laugh at them while they searched, but there was no tell-tale sniggering or scent of disturbed mud coming from the undergrowth. He must have chosen another place to hide this time.

She sniffed the ground and stood up. It wasn't cheating to follow her friends' scent—part of the game was to try to disguise your trail. She could tell that Dasher, Roller, and Jumper had all run in one direction, and Chomper had split off almost immediately and doubled back to head the other way. She decided to follow Chomper's trail first.

As she made her way through the forest, sniffing under rocks and listening to the pattern of leaves shifting in the wind, she couldn't help thinking about what Aunt Plum was doing now. It was going to be Dying Light soon. She had been away for twelve feasts. Had she managed to find food for all of them? How far had she made it up the mountain? Was she still in the forest, or was she already climbing the bare crags that made up the roots of the White Spine Mountains? Was she cold?

Leaf shook herself and tried to focus on the game. It was a much safer distraction than the disastrous attempt to cross the river—which she had not mentioned to the rest of the Slenderwood pandas—but it was also less effective. No matter how much attention she paid to the pattern of paw prints in a patch of mud or the dark corners underneath bushes, it wasn't enough to stop her from worrying.

Except . . . What was that lump under that pile of leaves? Had it moved?

She crept toward it, pretending not to see it, until she was standing right beside the leaves. Then she huffed in pretend frustration and turned her back.

Sure enough, there was a soft giggle from behind her.

Leaf spun around and patted her paw gently on the giggling lump.

"I found Chomper Digging Deep!" she declared. The lump wriggled under her paw, and Chomper stood up, shaking the leaves off her fur.

"Good finding," she said cheerily. "Want me to help look for the others?"

"Sure," Leaf said, and they set off together back the way she'd come. It was easier not to think of Plum with Chomper bounding at her side. Eventually they came upon a tall stand of pine trees, and Leaf froze as she heard something high above her head. She couldn't see anything through the thick needles, but something had moved.

"Could be a bird," Chomper muttered. "But I can sneak up the next tree along. If there's someone up there, I'll catch them!"

"Yes," Leaf agreed. "And I'll wait down here in case they try to swap hiding places on us." Changing your hiding place was against the rules, but it was the kind of rule that everyone agreed was more fun to break sometimes.

Chomper scampered up a nearby tree trunk and disappeared into the canopy, and Leaf began pretending to nose around in the undergrowth, in case the hiding red panda above her was watching.

Suddenly, she spotted something a little way away. A

distinctive striped tail, sticking out from behind another tree. Leaf grinned to herself and crept up to it, ready to spring and surprise whichever of her friends it was who'd been so careless.

But as she drew nearer, she scented something that made her paw steps falter and stop.

It was blood.

Feeling sick, she followed the scent closer and closer, treading a wide circle around the tree. More of the panda came into view slowly, as if in a horrible dream—the tail, the back legs, and then . . .

The front legs and the head were some distance away, and in the middle there was just a red, chewed-up mess.

Leaf stumbled back, turning her head and closing her eyes. Her stomach roiled, and for a long moment she couldn't make herself look again. But eventually the forest stopped spinning around her, and she did look.

The red panda had been eaten. And now that she was closer, she could smell the scent of a predator on the ground around it—the scent of fur and dead things.

Leaf startled as she heard the rustle and scamper of paws in the tree above her. Her friends were still playing their game, with no idea that one of their family had been killed. Her heart hurt as she heard Chomper's cry ring out from the trees above: "I found Dasher Climbing Far!"

With a skitter and a crash, Chomper and Dasher both leaped down from the branches of the tree. Dasher was picking pine needles out of his fur.

"That was a bad hiding place," he said. "Remind me not to pick a pine tree again."

"Dasher," Leaf said in a small voice, but her friend didn't seem to hear her. She swallowed and backed away from the red panda's body, threw her head back, and roared to the sky. "Stop the finding! Something's happened!"

Dasher and Chomper scampered over to her and skidded to a halt as they saw what she was looking at.

"Great Dragon!" Chomper exclaimed, sinking to her belly and putting her paws over her eyes. Dasher padded warily toward the dead red panda. He brushed against Leaf as he passed, and the gesture made Leaf feel a little steadier, although not very much.

"Oh no," he croaked. "It's Scratcher."

Leaf's heart ached for Dasher. Scratcher was a Climbing Far, one of Dasher's extended family—an uncle, she thought, or maybe a cousin.

"I'll go and tell the others," Chomper said, and vanished into the trees. Dasher padded back to Leaf and curled up between her paws, tucking his tail over his nose.

"What do you think did this?" he asked, in a muffled voice.

"I don't know," said Leaf. She gave the top of his head a gentle lick. "Maybe a leopard came down from the mountains. Or a brown bear. But I don't know."

They waited there for a little while, until Chomper returned with a group of Climbing Fars and other red pandas trailing behind her. They gathered around the body of Scratcher, sniffing and letting out keening wails of grief.

Dasher's mother, Seeker, ran over to him and Leaf and curled her tail comfortingly around his shoulders. There was a crunching of twigs behind them, and then Gale and Crabapple Slenderwood appeared too.

"We heard the noise," Gale said. Crabapple sat down heavily as he saw the body, and let out a deep sigh.

"So there's a predator in the forest," he said.

"Leopards," growled Jumper, who had arrived with the rest of the Climbing Fars. "Must be."

"Or wolves," said Racer Climbing Far, with a heavy shudder. "There are wolves in the mountains. And foxes."

Gale edged closer. She sniffed once at the bloodied body of Scratcher and then stood back.

"Leopard or wolf, maybe," she said. "But whatever it was . . . it was big. The tooth marks are . . . well, they're *big*."

There was a heavy pause. The assembled creatures all looked around nervously.

"Oh, Great Dragon," keened one of the red pandas, holding Scratcher's limp tail between her paws. "Why have you forsaken us?"

"The Dragon has deserted us," echoed another Climbing Far.

"It hasn't!" Leaf snapped. "I'm sorry about Scratcher. But Plum has gone to the Dragon's cave; she'll find the answer there. I know she will."

She looked to the other pandas for backup, but to her dismay neither Gale nor Crabapple would meet her eyes.

Leaf swallowed stiffly. *Oh, Aunt Plum . . . your mission might be even more urgent than we thought.*

"Now, Climbing Fars," said Seeker, standing up on her hind legs. "We can't let this predator frighten us into blaming the Dragon. We'll hold the vigil, like we do for any red panda who leaves us. Come along." She padded over and gently pulled the crying red panda away from Scratcher's tail. "Let go, Racer. That's right. Predators are a part of life, like any other. And Scratcher had a good life, didn't he?"

Leaf guessed that Racer must have been Scratcher's mate. She sagged to the ground with a faint yowl, and then let the other Climbing Fars help her start to climb the tree. Leaf had heard Dasher talk about the vigil before. The whole extended family would climb to the tops of the trees and stay there until Golden Light the next day, watching the stars and thinking about the life of the red panda they'd lost.

Gale and Crabapple retreated quietly, leaving the red pandas to their vigil. Leaf gave Dasher a last nuzzle on the top of his head, then stood back to let him climb the tree with his family. Before he turned away, he looked up at her, and there was determination in his eyes.

"Those squirrels are wrong," he said quietly to Leaf. "We *need* to find a way over the river. Now more than ever. If there's a huge predator in the Northern Forest, we need to have somewhere to go." He looked at his mother. "I'll be back before the vigil starts, but I want to go with Leaf to the river right now."

Seeker nodded solemnly. "That's all right. Just... be careful.

*Really*, this time. Don't go testing out any floating trees today."

Leaf felt a little guilty that Dasher had told his family about the incident with the bamboo but she hadn't told hers. Dasher promised his mother they wouldn't do anything too risky, and they set off toward the river.

They walked up and down the bank between Long Light and Sun Fall. Dasher didn't break his word, but for the first time, he seemed just as desperate as Leaf to find a way across.

"Maybe this one," he said, putting his front paws on a dead tree that was floating tangled in reeds and giving it a shove. It moved a little. "We could chew through these reeds, and you could push it out into the river. I reckon it'd hold us both."

"But then we'd just be floating downstream again," Leaf pointed out gently. "What we need is something we can use to get straight across. Maybe if there was a long enough piece of ivy, or . . ."

"Still trying to cross the river?" chittered a voice from above. Leaf sighed and looked up to see the same two flying squirrels sitting on a branch above her head.

"We told you," said the other one. "Not good listeners, are you, pandas?"

"They used to be so wise," said the first, addressing its friend as if Leaf and Dasher weren't even there. "What happened to them? Don't they teach their cubs how to save their own hides anymore?"

"Hey!" Dasher growled. "Leave her alone—at least we're trying!"

"Seems as if they're useless without their Dragon Speaker," the squirrel went on, ignoring Dasher completely.

"*Hey!*" he barked again. "You shut up about the pandas! Or I'll come up there and—"

"Maybe we'd better go," Leaf said, putting her body between Dasher and the squirrels' tree. "We can try again another time. You've got to get back, remember?" She lowered her voice. "I don't care what these little idiots say. I know the Dragon is with us, and we're doing our best. Come on."

She nudged him with her nose until he gave up and let himself be pushed away.

"Sorry," Dasher said. "It's just, after what happened to Scratcher . . . we ought to be looking for a way to get away from that predator, not being insulted by squirrels."

"We'll be okay," Leaf reassured him as they walked. "The predator might have just been passing through. Something that big might be a long way away by now."

"Perhaps *it* tried to cross the river," Dasher said, brightening a little.

Suddenly there was a rustling up ahead, and the brightness faded at once. Leaf felt her own skin prickle as the bushes shook, but before she could say anything, a flock of bright red birds burst out, making straight for them. They were golden pheasants, and they were running in a headlong charge that would have been a stampede if they'd been bigger creatures, their yellow heads bobbing on their striped necks, long brown speckled tails flapping as they trampled the leaves. They split around Leaf and Dasher as if the two friends were rocks in the stream of the river, squawking in panic.

Leaf barely had time to feel relieved that the birds weren't a flock of predators before a horrible realization struck her.

*Something's coming.*

"Get up in the tree!" she snapped to Dasher, and ran to the nearest trunk herself. Dasher was right behind her, scrambling up with his quick, small steps. He ran out onto the branches, hopping between them until he was hidden in a thick patch of leaves, his tail curled tightly around the branch behind him. Leaf kept climbing the trunk, using every claw hold she could find. A scent began to filter through on the breeze, and she held her breath and climbed faster. The scent of death.

*The predator. It's here.*

She finally found a solid split in the trunk, high off the ground, and dared to stop and look down, trying to keep perfectly still. She couldn't see Dasher now. She just hoped he was still hidden from below. . . .

Then she saw it.

Leaf had seen a leopard before—only once, and from some distance—as it came down from the White Spine, with its long tail and thick spotted fur.

This predator was like a leopard, but also completely different. It moved in the same sort of graceful way, but it was much bigger and sleeker, with fur that didn't hide its powerful muscles as it stalked through the forest. It was striped, not spotted, and its stripes were black and orange, as bright as the neck feathers on the golden pheasants, or even brighter.

Despite the obvious power in its movements, the creature

was absolutely silent as it padded under the tree where Leaf and Dasher were hiding. Terror gripped Leaf as she realized that if it hadn't been for the pheasants, she would never have known it was here until it was almost on her. The scent was strong, but it would have come too late.

*Poor Scratcher might not even have known what was happening until that monster had him in its teeth,* she thought.

Right underneath the tree, the creature paused, one front paw lifted mid-step. It turned its head this way and that, black-lined ears swiveling, and raised its muzzle a little, scenting the air with a twitch of its long white whiskers.

Leaf's heart was hammering, and she was afraid that her breathing would be loud enough to give her away.

*Can it climb trees?* she wondered in a panic.

Then the creature put down its paw and walked on. Leaf tried not to breathe again until she had lost sight of it in the trees, and even after it was gone she couldn't bring herself to move for another few long moments.

Finally, she saw Dasher emerge from his leaves and climb the trunk up to meet her. He clung to the branch beside her, and they just looked at each other in dismay.

"Nobody's safe," Leaf said eventually. "Not with that thing on the prowl. We have to do something."

# CHAPTER NINE

GHOST WATCHED THE MOUNTAIN goats grazing on the bushes, seemingly unbothered by the steepness of the crag where they had found the greenery growing up through a thin dusting of snow. Their big curly horns bobbed as they nibbled.

They were much, much bigger than the hare that Frost and Snowstorm had caught before. If they could bring one down, it would feed the whole family for days and days.

Ghost felt strangely positive about the idea of catching one of the goats. The hare was fast and could vanish into the snow before Ghost could get close, but it would take strength as well as speed to hunt one of these woolly creatures. And his litter-mates might be able to avoid being struck by the horns, but he was the one who could wrestle it to the ground.

All four cubs Born of Winter were huddled behind a sticking-out rock, carefully staying downwind of the herd, watching the goats with hungry eyes.

*And what better way to show Icebound and her stupid cubs that I do belong here?* he thought. He knew he ought to just ignore them, but part of him wanted to bring the biggest, grumpiest-looking goat in the herd back to Winter's cave. That would show them all that he was as good a leopard as any other.

But it wasn't the smart thing to do.

"That one," he whispered to the other cubs. "The lowest down the slope, trying to eat the leaves off that spiky bush."

It was thin, compared to the others, but it would still make a good meal for a leopard family. It looked elderly: the sparse and straggly hair on its back had leaves and twigs caught in it. Its legs even wobbled a little as it shifted around on the steep rocks to try to get a better angle on the bush's leaves. Now it was facing away from the cubs.

Ghost heard Winter's voice in his head.

*When the chance comes to pounce, don't wait.*

He had to go. *Now.*

He exploded from behind the rock, kicking back a shower of pebbles.

"What in the Snow Cat's—Ghost, wait!" he heard Snowstorm hiss behind him, but it was too late now. He was charging across the cliff, eyes locked on the goat's flank. He had to make it, before . . .

But it was too far, and the scattering pebbles had been too loud. The goat turned, saw him coming, and yelled a warning to the others.

"Snow Cat's *teeth,*" Ghost heard Frost snap, and then the

other three cubs bounded out from their hiding place after him.

Ghost tried to focus on the elderly goat. He could still make it. . . .

The goat reared up and turned on its back legs, and in that moment Ghost realized he had misjudged the creature. It might be elderly, but it wasn't as infirm as it looked. It kicked off and bounded away across the slope in great, steady leaps, while Ghost had to slow to pick his way across the treacherous rocks. The others raced past him, but the whole herd was scattering, bleating their fright to the sky, and to any other prey that might be close by too. A whole flock of sparrows took flight from one of the trees and circled overhead, cheeping madly.

Snowstorm came closest to catching one of the goats, rocketing across the uneven ground, her teeth snapping audibly just shy of one of their legs. But then they were gone, and even the normal cubs couldn't keep their footing well enough to follow them along the crag.

"Ghost!" Frost stumbled to a halt and yowled. "Why did you do that?"

"I thought I could get it," Ghost muttered. "Mother said not to miss a chance to pounce. I thought I could make it."

Frost rolled his eyes. "Yes, but she meant—"

He broke off and gave a hard sigh, treading the rocks with his paws.

Ghost felt cold. He knew exactly what his brother had been about to say.

*She meant us, not you. That advice is for normal cubs. You were always going to mess this up.*

He didn't bother to challenge Frost. Both of them knew what he meant. He just turned and walked up the slope, hoping against hope that there might be more prey elsewhere that hadn't been spooked away by the goats' panic.

"Ghost," Snowstorm called after him. "It's no good. Let's go home. They won't graze here again for a long time. It's all right," she added. Ghost screwed up his face and dug his claws into the cracks between the rocks.

It wasn't all right. He would never learn to hunt. Either he would stay with Winter for the rest of his life, being fed like a cub from the prey she caught, or he would starve.

But Snowstorm was trying to be kind. He turned back and headed for home without another word.

"Ghost, come inside," Shiver meowed. Ghost turned and saw her faint shape standing at the mouth of the cave. The other three cubs had been snoozing in the den with Winter, but Ghost had told them he needed air, and had gone to sit outside by himself. Now it was snowing heavily, even on the sheltered slope by the cave, and the sun was setting somewhere far away behind the thick banks of cloud. Drifts were piling up against the rocks and a thin, perfect blanket of white covered the ground and the trees.

"It's not as warm inside without you," Shiver complained. Ghost knew that wasn't true; she wanted him to come back inside because she could tell he was upset. But he couldn't.

"Just a bit longer," he said. "I'll come in soon."

Shiver gave a worried half growl. "Please do. It's cold out here."

"I'm not cold. Go back to sleep," Ghost replied, trying to sound reassuring.

Shiver hesitated, then turned and padded back inside the cave.

Ghost felt relieved when she wasn't watching him anymore, but the relief soon faded and the anxiety rose again like a flood, until it threatened to drown him.

*What am I going to do? What can I do to get better?*

He was so afraid that the answer was *nothing—you can only make things worse.* He didn't want to ever move from this spot again, because at least if he sat here, perfectly still, he couldn't ruin anything else for his littermates.

The wind died suddenly, and the snow slowed and then stopped altogether. The light that had been gray and feeble was almost gone now. Ghost gazed up at the sky, where the clouds still swirled, dark gray and overpowering. Every so often they would part to reveal dark sky behind, and Ghost would glimpse a few glimmering stars before the clouds closed over them again.

Ghost waited until he could fix his gaze on a single bright star, like the gleam in a giant eye, and then he spoke quietly.

"Snow Cat, please," he said. "I just want to be a good leopard. Please, help me."

He suddenly felt a warm gust of air pass over the back of his neck, as if a huge creature had breathed gently on his fur.

He spun around, but there was nothing there. But the warm air kept flowing past him, almost seeming to wrap around him, like Winter used to wrap her tail right around him when he was just a tiny cub. Then the snow began to glow, faintly and then brighter and brighter. Ghost blinked, not sure what he was seeing. Was he going crazy? Then he looked up. The clouds were parting slowly, revealing a sky scattered with shimmering stars. Their light made the snow on the ground glitter and shine. It was so beautiful that Ghost didn't immediately notice the shapes in the snow. They led from the rock he was sitting on, winding toward a copse of trees that grew farther down the mountain. They looked like depressions in the snow, dark and clear against the glittering starlight, as if some enormous creature had walked across the rocks, its paws melting the snow behind it. Ghost took a few hesitant steps forward. The marks definitely led toward the copse, but they seemed to end there. . . .

Then the clouds parted again, and the moon came out. It flooded the landscape with bright, clear, ordinary moonlight.

And the marks were gone.

"*What?*" Ghost bounded forward again, to a spot where he *knew* he had seen the trail, but the snow was clear and perfect.

Ghost's heart began to beat, faster and faster.

"Snow Cat," he breathed. "Leave your paw prints in the snow, that we may follow them. That's what we always say. And . . . and you *did!*"

He took another long look at the copse on the mountain slope below, trying to fix in his mind the exact position where he'd seen the marks vanish, and then he turned and ran back to the cave.

"Mother," he said as he skidded inside. "Something's happened. Something *amazing* has happened!"

"Ghost," Winter replied. "What do you mean? I'm glad you've come inside—"

"You have to come! You all have to come. The Snow Cat sent me a sign!"

Snowstorm and Frost raised their heads and blinked blearily at him.

"You . . . What?" Snowstorm stood up and shook herself from ears to tail. "The Snow Cat did *what?*"

"I saw its prints in the snow," Ghost gasped. "Just like we always ask it! One minute there was nothing there—the snow was fresh, just like it is now—and then I felt its breath on me, and then I *saw* them, leading down to the trees, farther down the slope. We've got to follow!"

Frost and Snowstorm stared at Ghost, then looked at each other, and then at Winter.

"Wow," Shiver whispered. "Show me!"

Ghost's fur felt almost as warm as when the Snow Cat had breathed on him with its breath. He'd known Shiver would understand. He led her back outside. She looked out onto the snow, her eyes huge and round in the moonlight, and then she looked up at Ghost in disappointment.

"I don't see anything," she said.

"No, they vanished again when the moon came out," Ghost said. "But I know exactly where they were leading."

"*Ghost*, come on," Snowstorm said, stepping out of the cave with Frost and Winter in tow. "There's nothing there, and there's clearly never been anything there. Maybe you dozed off. Or it was a trick of the moonlight."

Ghost started to shrink into himself, and then changed his mind and sat up tall and straight. "I don't care what you think. I saw them, and I'm going."

"We'll all go," said Winter firmly. She turned to Snowstorm, who gave her a pleading look, and Frost, who just looked totally confused. "We believe in Ghost, don't we? So we'll follow the Snow Cat's path and see where it leads us."

Ghost gave his mother a quick, grateful nuzzle and then turned and headed away at a fast trot across the snow, with Shiver scurrying at his heels.

It felt good to be leading the way, even if he wasn't quite sure what he was leading the way to.

*Please, Snow Cat,* he thought, looking down at Shiver's expectant face, and back at the skeptical expressions of his other littermates. *Please don't fail me now. . . .*

They drew close to the copse of trees, where Ghost had seen the marks in the snow vanish, and he slowed and stopped. Something told him not to go into the trees just yet. There was nothing there now but darkness and the scent of pine needles. He led his family instead to a sheltered spot behind a large patch of grass, and gestured them to stay put and wait. He settled down, his heart beating hard in his throat, and watched the trees keenly.

*What if we're too late?* he thought. *What if I was supposed to go at once, and not fetch the others?*

Nothing happened for what felt like a long, long time. Snowstorm and Frost had started out keeping obediently still and silent, as if they sensed that something was about to happen, but finally Frost rested his chin affectionately on Ghost's shoulder and said, "You're *sure* you saw something? Don't you think you might have imagined it?"

"I . . . *no*," Ghost whispered back. "It was like a dream, but I was awake. It was *real*."

*But perhaps I was wrong about what it meant,* he thought. *Perhaps I should have gone straight into the trees. Perhaps . . .*

Then there was a crunching of pine needles, and the scent of cracked pine and . . .

Prey!

Ghost peered between the long blades of grass and saw a large deer step delicately out of the trees and into the moonlight. It looked around, ears pricked and huge black eyes alert. Then it turned its back on the leopards and lowered its head to graze on the grasses around the base of the trees.

He looked around and saw with satisfaction that Snowstorm's and Frost's jaws were open in shock. Shiver kneaded the snow at her paws with excitement.

"Can you catch it?" she breathed to Ghost.

Ghost looked at the deer. It was oblivious to their presence, just like the goat. Then he looked at his mother. Winter was watching him carefully, her gaze occasionally flicking back to the deer.

"I can't," Ghost said. "But you can, can't you, Mother?"

Winter pressed her forehead to his. "Good boy," she said, so low he was sure the others couldn't even hear. "I love you." Then she turned to the others. "Stay here." And she stepped out from behind the grass without hesitation, moving fast, but in absolute silence. Ghost and his littermates could only huddle close together and watch as Winter stalked closer and closer to the deer, her belly low to the ground and her haunches tense. As soon as she was close enough, she leaped. The deer never knew what was coming until it was on the ground, spindly legs kicking in the air, with Winter's fangs buried deep in its neck.

Ghost sprang from the bush and ran over to her, with his littermates on his heels.

"Ghost," Winter said, looking up at him, the deer's blood painting her muzzle a deep dark red in the moonlight. "Go on. It's your kill."

Ghost lowered his jaw to the neck of the weakly struggling creature and bit down as hard as he could. The deer went limp almost at once.

"It's a feast!" Shiver meowed, pacing from one end of the deer's body to the other, sniffing happily. "Well done, Ghost!"

Winter bowed her head. "Let's say the blessing, everyone."

"We thank the Snow Cat for giving us this prey," chorused all four leopards. "May you leave your paw prints in the snow, that we may follow them."

"And thank you for leaving your paw prints that Ghost could follow them!" Shiver added at the end.

"Sorry we didn't believe you," Snowstorm said. "But, you

know . . . that doesn't *happen*." She looked confused, as if she still didn't actually believe it. "The Snow Cat doesn't *actually* show us where to go; it's just a blessing."

"It was real tonight," said Winter softly. "I've always known how special Ghost was. It appears that the Snow Cat knows it too. Now let's eat our fill, and we can bring what we haven't finished to the cave when we're done."

"Wow! Leftovers!" cried Shiver, rearing up on her back paws and sinking her teeth into the deer carcass in such a playful way that Ghost burst out laughing.

He ate alongside his family, under the moonlight, filling his hungry belly with warm and sustaining meat.

The Snow Cat had shown him his place, and it was here, in the mountains, hunting with his mother.

He couldn't remember ever feeling happier.

# CHAPTER TEN

"I'M GONNA GET YOU," Rain muttered, watching the swirling carp. If she stood perfectly still in the water, the fish seemed to forget that she was a panda and not some kind of black-and-white fuzzy rock. They weren't very clever creatures—strange, since they were supposed to be favored by the Great Dragon, and catching one could give you luck for a whole season.

Rain told herself she wasn't lurking. She was playing with the carp. But perhaps it wasn't *pure* coincidence that she had chosen a strip of shallow water some distance from the waterfall. She didn't want to be able to hear it. Her dream had been so incredibly vivid that now when she heard its persistent, pleasant burbling sound, a part of her could almost hear it starting to turn into a roar.

"Why did I dream about a three-headed dragon, anyway?" she asked the carp as they circled closer and closer. "I bet

Pebble would tell me it was a message from the Great Dragon. But why did it have three heads? Stupid dragon. Doesn't even make sense in my imagination."

She waited another few heartbeats, enjoying the gentle splashing of the river and the sounds of birds and smaller creatures going about their business in the forest behind her. The carp came even closer, and she slowly lowered herself into the water, still pretending to be a mossy rock, until the moment came and she put her head down and dived. The carp swiveled and swam apart, but Rain was quick, and she had already chosen her target: a big, fat, golden fish with patterns of white on its scales. She kept her eyes on that carp and swam, one, two, three strong strokes until it was within reach of her jaws. She grabbed it and splashed to the surface, triumphantly holding the wriggling fish.

"Nice catch," said a voice.

Rain spun around, splashing in the water.

Sunset Deepwood was sitting on the riverbank, watching her.

"Uh. Thanks." Rain had been thinking about eating the fish this time, but it seemed wrong to chomp on it in front of the Dragon Speaker, when it wasn't even time for a feast.

*You win again, lucky fish,* she thought, releasing it into the river. It was gone in a flash of golden scales.

"I'm impressed, but I'm also disappointed," Sunset said. "It's a shame you left the search party so early."

Rain bristled, and slowly began to walk back to shore. She wanted to be out of the water, but she didn't want to give him the impression that she was hurrying for his sake.

"How do you know when I left?" she asked. A flash of mischief seized her. "Surely you didn't use the Seeing Stone for something so trivial?" She pulled herself up onto a flat rock and sat down, casually scratching at her belly.

To her slight surprise, Sunset laughed. "Very good," he said. "You are a clever panda, aren't you? No, nothing like that. Pebble told me."

"He's back?" Rain sat up straighter. "Already?"

"Oh yes. His was the first search party to return."

"But why?" Rain frowned. "He and Blossom were really excited. Why did they come home so soon?"

"Because they succeeded," said Sunset, and Rain's jaw dropped, just a little.

"You don't mean—they didn't find—not *Stone?*"

"No." Sunset's slightly smug expression turned sad for a moment. "No, I'm afraid Pebble's brother is still among the missing. But they found a young cub, younger than you, wandering in the wilderness. His mother died just recently, and he'd been fending for himself, poor thing. But that is somewhat beside the point," he said, fixing Rain with a keen, slightly amused stare. "I came here to talk about *you*. Pebble explained what had happened. He told me I would probably find you here."

Rain snorted crossly. She wished Pebble hadn't told him that. Between this and her strange feelings about the waterfall, the number of places on the river that felt completely *hers* was shrinking fast.

"I understand why you volunteered," Sunset said. "You wanted to help your friend. That's very admirable, Rain. I'm not sure you really understand how brave that was of you."

Rain frowned. She didn't know why being complimented by this panda annoyed her so much.

*Maybe,* said a voice in her head that sounded a lot like Pebble, *you don't actually need to be annoyed. Maybe he's actually trying to be nice.*

"And I understand why you left the mission, too," Sunset went on.

"Oh yeah?" Had Pebble told him *everything*? Did he know that she was suspicious of him, that she didn't even think she believed in the Great Dragon?

"You're an independent-minded panda," said Sunset. "I'm sure you didn't enjoy following Blossom's lead. You were never suited to such a group effort."

". . . Oh." Rain had to admit, he might have a point there.

"You would have done well in the old days, when we all lived far apart, and only came together when the need for company was particularly great. But those days are gone, Rain. The era of pandas working together is here. The Great Dragon has shown me that this is the truth. So." He got up and paced to the very edge of the water, putting his front paws in and letting the river lap at them. "When I heard that you liked to swim—and when I saw you catch that carp, and saw how fast and strong you are in the water—I had an idea. I have a special mission, just for you. When I say we need to reunite all pandas, I mean those who live in the Northern Forest, too. There may be pandas there who need our help. We must find a way to reach them. And I believe if any panda can conquer the river these days, it's you."

"You're flattering me so I'll do what you want," Rain said bluntly. Sunset blinked placidly up at her.

"Is it working?" he asked with a kind smile. "It's all true, by the way. You really are the best panda for this task. And we really *must* find all the missing pandas, not just the ones it's easy for us to find."

"Nobody can cross the river," Rain said. She turned to look across at the Northern Forest, beyond the rapid, churning current. "Or someone would have done it by now."

The fish was back. It swam up to the surface, nibbling on a clump of algae. Rain watched it glide about, oblivious to the two pandas on the shore. *If Sunset is up to something*, she thought, *this could be my chance to find out what.*

She looked back at Sunset. "But I'll try. I'll find a way across the river, if you want."

Sunset gave a deep bow. "Thank you, Rain. I hope that this way, you'll realize how satisfying it is to serve your fellow pandas—we each just need to find the best way for us to do that. I believe the Great Dragon will guide you, and you will find the way you seek."

He walked away into the forest, and Rain watched him go, tapping her claws thoughtfully on her rock.

*What have I gotten myself into?*

When Rain returned to the clearing for the Feast of Dying Light, she found Peony, Dawn, and Azalea gathered around a small, skinny pile of black-and-white fluff. As she watched, the cub ate his way through half a bamboo stalk, and then curled up between Azalea and Dawn and fell into a restless sleep.

"His name's Maple," Peony said to Rain. "Oh, he's so weak. Pebble and Blossom only just found him in time."

She didn't say anything about Rain leaving the search party, but from the way she said Pebble's and Blossom's names, it was clear she knew. Rain felt guilty for not coming clean earlier. Sunset Deepwood was one thing—she didn't really care what he thought of her—but she felt Peony's silent disappointment like a thorn in the ribs.

She spotted Pebble on the other side of the clearing, talking to Mist and Squall, and hurried over.

"Hey, Pebble," she said. He turned, and Rain saw that her best friend looked worn out. "I—I hear you saved that cub's life. What happened?"

She hoped that would serve as an apology, but Pebble's expression turned cloudy.

"So you admit it. It's not all just some trick. There really are pandas out there who need our help."

Rain glanced back at the skinny form of Maple. He was snoring.

"I know, I . . . I got it wrong. I'm . . . sorry."

Pebble gave her a slightly skeptical look, and Rain cringed. She really meant it! She was sorry! It wasn't her fault that saying it out loud felt like trying to push a mountain through a hollow bamboo cane.

"I accept your apology," Pebble said stiffly.

"And I hope we find Stone," Rain added. "I really, really do. I'm sorry if I made it sound like I didn't care about him."

Pebble nodded. "Thanks," he said.

And then he turned and walked away from her. Rain watched him go in dismay.

*I apologized. And I meant it. Why isn't it okay?*

Rain lay in her bed of moss and reeds, staring up at the stars. They seemed to wink and shift as she watched, wisps of dark cloud covering one part of the sky and then another.

The pandas all slept in nests dotted up and down the same slope, far enough apart that they didn't need to talk, but close enough that they could. Rain's nest was a comfy little shelf of grassy earth exactly the right size for one panda to lie down upon, with a good view through the trees to the river. Usually she loved to lie in her nest and watch the stars or listen to the distant splash of water. But tonight she couldn't seem to get comfortable. Perhaps Frog and Fir had put pine cones in her nest as revenge for her pretending to be a Dragon Speaker all those times? But when she nosed around, she couldn't find anything that shouldn't be there.

Pebble's nest was just down the slope, in a hollow underneath an overhanging rock. When Rain couldn't sleep, she would sometimes climb down there and bother him. Or when it was raining. But she couldn't do that, either.

*Before Sunset came back, I slept like a log. I didn't have any strange worries about monkeys; I didn't have weird dreams about dragons made of steam. And Pebble was still talking to me.*

The soft sounds of pandas snoring reverberated across the slope. None of the others seemed to be having any problem sleeping.

But then there was another sound, coming from somewhere up the hill. A rasping, squeaky voice.

"Big strong panda," it said, in a mocking, singsong tone. "Big brave panda."

Rain leaped to her feet.

*That's Brawnshanks!* She was sure it was, and the laughter that followed was unmistakably the annoying chittering of a whole troop of monkeys. *What are they up to now?*

She started to climb, over rocks and between trees, trying to follow the route that would make the least noise, without tripping over any of the sleeping pandas. She could soon see where the voices must be coming from—a clump of short trees where the branches were moving as if in a gale, though the air was still.

"Where's your mother, big brave panda?" Brawnshanks's voice snarled, and Rain's heart squeezed in her chest as she heard a faint, hoarse voice reply.

"She d-died. In a rockfall."

*Was that Maple?*

She crept closer until she could see between the trees. The monkeys were leaping from branch to branch, moving all the time, sometimes jumping down to the ground, sometimes swinging wildly from their tails in the tops of the trees. And right in the middle of them, trapped and shivering, was the little cub who Pebble had brought back with him.

"And you were all alone." Brawnshanks landed on the ground right in front of Maple and prodded him hard in his skinny chest with one long, leathery finger. The monkeys let out another chittering laugh, and anger began to heat the back of Rain's neck. "Or *were* you? What about your siblings?"

"I . . . I don't have any siblings," stammered Maple.

"You *do*. You have *two*. Isn't that *right*?" With each word, Brawnshanks gave Maple a shove, first one way and then another.

"No!" Maple yelped. "Please let me go! I don't have any siblings! Please, I—I want my mother. . . ." He broke down into keening cries, and Rain couldn't take it anymore. She burst from the undergrowth and charged right into the middle of the trees, shoving one monkey aside and scattering the rest. They screeched and chattered at her as they leaped out of the way.

"Who's this?"

"Stupid big panda, mind your own business!"

Rain put her head down and head-butted Brawnshanks right in the stomach, sending him flying onto his back.

"Leave Maple alone, you nasty little bullies!" she snarled, baring her teeth at them. "What are you doing to him?"

"None of your business," Brawnshanks sneered, getting to his paws and leaping up into the trees to hang upside down, just out of reach of Rain's claws.

"Maple, get behind me," Rain ordered. The cub let out a worried whine and scampered behind her, pressing his shoulder against her flank.

"We're not finished," Brawnshanks said, snarling to show off his teeth too—tiny, compared to Rain's, but razor sharp.

"Yes, you are!" boomed another voice. Rain spun around to see Sunset pounding up the slope, a furious look on his face. "You moneys dare to come here and treat one of our young this way? You there," he said to Brawnshanks, "if you are their leader, you'll do what's best for your troop and go far away, and leave us in peace!"

*If you are their leader . . .*

Rain stared at Sunset as he squared up to Brawnshanks. The look Brawnshanks returned him was amused, but not the aggressive, sneering amusement he'd shown Rain.

*You know each other. This . . . this rescue is a lie.*

But she couldn't let Sunset know that she knew. She backed away, keeping Maple pressed close to her side, while Sunset growled at the monkey he *knew* was called Brawnshanks.

"Let's go," Brawnshanks howled, and the monkeys hopped and swung away, scattering across the ground and up into trees.

"Thank goodness you found them in time," Sunset said, turning to Rain as the last golden hide slipped from sight. He lowered his muzzle to address Maple. "My poor cub, are you all right?"

Maple couldn't seem to speak at all. He pressed himself even closer to Rain's flank and managed to nod stiffly.

"Come, little one," Sunset said. "We will protect you."

With gentle encouragement, he managed to get Maple

walking, and the two of them started to descend the slope toward the panda nests. Rain let them walk in front, but kept close all the way to the nest where Dawn, Frog, and Fir were curled up together. She didn't want to let the skinny cub out of her sight until he was safe with good, normal pandas. Sunset helped Maple tuck himself in against them, and then bid him and Rain good night and walked away. Rain pretended to head back to her own nest, but instead she climbed a tree and watched as Sunset found his way to his mossy spot and lay down.

*This smells rotten.*

Sunset was a liar, and she had something like proof, even if no panda but her knew it. But what was it all *for*?

*I'm watching you, Sunset Deepwood.*

# CHAPTER ELEVEN

LEAF STRETCHED OUT, MAKING sure that her paws were firmly braced on a thick branch. Her back and neck crunched and clicked where they had stiffened from a cold night sleeping in the high crook of a gingko tree. It was satisfying, but she still ached afterward.

There were grunts and snorts from the other branches, and the leaves bounced and shook. All around her, the trees were full of stirring, uncomfortable pandas.

But they were all still alive. The Slenderwood pandas had made it through the night. In the faint gray light, the trees looked like they had sprouted huge, fluffy black-and-white and red fruits. The red pandas—Swimming Deeps and Digging Deeps, Leaping Highs, Healing Hearts, and others—had all joined the pandas in the trees, along with the Climbing Fars when their vigil ended. Dasher had come to find Leaf and curled up on top of her flank, his long, fluffy tail wrapped around them both for warmth until she had woken at Gray Light.

None of them had been taken by the slinking orange creature.

*Tiger.*

Leaf shuddered a little. When she and Dasher had returned to tell the Slenderwoods and the red pandas about what they'd seen, Juniper had told them he'd heard old tales of creatures that matched that description. The predator was a *tiger.*

Dasher's tail twitched against Leaf's nose and she looked around.

"You awake?" she whispered.

"Hnn." Dasher's eyes blinked open. "I am now."

"Sorry," Leaf said. "I need to get up. It's time for the First Feast."

"S'okay." Dasher got stiffly to his paws and climbed into a smaller crook of the tree to let Leaf get up.

"What's happening?" One of the other red pandas was stirring on a branch just below her.

"It's the Feast of Gray Light," Dasher explained. "The pandas need to eat."

"What, *now*?" The red panda squinted up at Leaf. "It's not even dawn yet!"

"No," Leaf agreed. "That would be the Feast of Golden Light."

"How many feasts are there?"

"Nine."

The red panda looked bleakly at Leaf, and then at Dasher, who nodded his confirmation. The other red panda turned around on his branch and curled up again, throwing his tail over his face.

Leaf sighed. The feast might disrupt the red pandas' sleep a little, but there was nothing she could do about it. They couldn't *not* have the feast, after all. That would be madness. Nothing could stop the Nine Feasts, not even a tiger.

Although, as she scanned the ground below, worry crept into her heart. There wasn't much bamboo in this part of the forest, even less than the Slenderwood's usual meager crop. If they couldn't find any at all, they would have to make do with the gingko fruit, and it would be a miserable start to a difficult day. . . .

"I see some!" yelled a high-pitched panda voice. Leaf cringed as red pandas all around her stirred and growled, but followed the voice hopefully. It was little Cane, of course, and by the time Leaf had climbed across the branches to the tree where he had been sleeping, he was already being gently chastised by Hyacinth to be quieter around their red-panda friends.

"Did you see bamboo?" Leaf asked. Cane nodded, his mouth pressed tightly shut, and pointed with one paw. Relief washed over Leaf as she followed his gesture and saw the bamboo—it was just one cane, but it grew tall and strong, and a bushy spray of leaves sprouted from its tip. Each Slenderwood panda would be able to have at least a good mouthful.

The only problem was that it stood too far from the tree for the pandas to reach over and grab the leaves for themselves.

"Some panda will have to go and get it," Hyacinth said quietly. "And that means going down onto the ground."

*Where the tiger could be lurking.* Whichever panda went down there would be vulnerable while they made the awkward climb back up the tree, more so because they'd be trying to hold on to a long bamboo cane at the same time.

"I'll go," Leaf said. "I'm the best climber; I'll be able to get back the fastest. It'll be no problem," she said, more brightly than she felt. "Can you watch my back?"

Hyacinth gave her a worried look, but nodded.

Leaf began to climb down the tree, staying in its branches as long as she could, even though some of them dipped dangerously under her weight, so that she would spend as little time on the ground as possible. All the way, she sniffed and listened for any hint of the tiger. There was no sign of it— but she remembered how smoothly and silently it had moved through the forest before. Just because she couldn't see it, that certainly didn't mean it wasn't there.

She reached the forest floor and hurried over to the bamboo and took the stem of it in her jaws.

There was no way to make this quiet. She would just have to be quick.

She snapped her jaws shut, using the full force of her bite for the first time in many feasts, and the crack of the bamboo echoed through the forest. In the Gray Light stillness, it sounded loud enough to wake the Dragon in its cave.

After tearing the cane from the ground, Leaf paused only long enough to make sure she had its heavy stem securely in her jaws, and then she ran back to the trunk of the nearest tree, dragging the bamboo behind her, and began to climb.

"Yeah!" Cane barked excitedly, before his mother shushed him again. Leaf kept climbing until she reached a strong, safe branch. She awkwardly yanked the bamboo up after her and wedged the thick end into a gap so that she could let go, and then she looked down.

Still no sign of the tiger.

"That was very brave," said Juniper, climbing across the tree branches toward her. "Plum would be proud. Why don't you say the blessing?"

Leaf smiled at him with pride, but the mention of Plum sent her heart dropping.

*She's out there alone, with a tiger on the prowl. Did she even make it to the mountains?*

But Leaf wouldn't let herself think like that. She had to believe that Plum was okay.

The pandas gathered around, and Leaf held the bamboo steady while they all picked bunches of leaves.

"Great Dragon, at the Feast of Gray Light your humble pandas bow before you. Thank you for the gift of the bamboo, and the wisdom you bestow upon us."

They all munched down on their feasts, a meager handful of leaves each, but Leaf thought it tasted extra fresh and delicious after all the trouble she had gone to collecting it. Afterward, Crabapple said, "I can't take many more nights like this." He dipped his head, and Leaf heard his neck crack.

"We're not all great climbers and tree-sleepers like you,

Leaf," Hyacinth agreed. "I was so afraid Cane would fall and hurt himself, I hardly slept a wink."

"I think we all know what we need to do," said Grass. "The Slenderwood is sparse, but at least it used to be safe. We must find a new territory."

"There *must* be somewhere that's got enough bamboo to feed us and isn't infested with tigers," Gale agreed.

*Leave the Slenderwood, forever?* Leaf stared down at the ground as this thought sank in. She couldn't deny Grass's and Gale's reasoning, but she couldn't imagine leaving, either. Where would they go?

"We're coming too," said a voice. Leaf looked up to the branches above her head and saw Seeker Climbing Far sitting with Splasher Swimming Deep, Hunter Leaping High, and a few others Leaf didn't know. "We talked about it during Scratcher's vigil," said Seeker. "We'll be better off if we stick together. You're all fearsome in a fight, if it comes to it, and we're quick and light on our feet and can provide many more eyes and ears in case the tiger comes back."

"Then it's decided," said Juniper. "We will move, all together."

"Wait!" Leaf gasped. "What about Plum? We can't just leave the Slenderwood without her! What if she comes back and doesn't know how to find us? Or she comes back and, instead of us, she finds that . . . that *thing*." She broke off with a shudder, trying not to imagine it.

"Yes, you're right," said Gale soothingly. "We must find Plum before we settle anywhere else."

"Then . . . let's head north, all together," said Hyacinth. "We'll find Plum, and—who knows?—maybe a new home is waiting for us on the higher slopes."

Leaf hoped so. She crunched on the stem of the bamboo as she listened to the pandas and the red pandas talk about the ideal territory they hoped to find. She still couldn't quite imagine it. The Slenderwood was the only home she had ever known. Would they really never come back to Grandfather Gingko and the riverbank and the Slenderwood clearing?

*Great Dragon, let us find Plum soon,* she thought. *I need her. . . .*

"Stop." Wanderer Leaping High held her tail up in the air, and the pandas all followed the signal and froze, scenting and listening intently. Red pandas advanced, some in the trees and some on the ground.

They had made good progress. The red pandas darted ahead as scouts, but always kept close enough to the pandas that they could run back if they met anything they needed to defend themselves against. They told the pandas the easiest ways around the hillsides, and the quickest, so they could decide which to take.

Already they were climbing a hillside in the Northern Forest where Leaf didn't think she had ever been before. All the way up and down the rolling slopes, bamboo grew about as sparsely as it had in the Slenderwood, enough for the pandas to make a meager feast as they passed through, but certainly not enough to warrant stopping for very long. The faint scent of predator still lingered on the air too, and whenever their noses caught it, without anyone saying the word *tiger*, all the pandas and red pandas walked a little faster.

"Okay," said Wanderer. "It's clear. Let's move on."

"It's nearly Long Light," said Gale. "We'll need to stop at the next patch of bamboo."

Wanderer sighed. She didn't say anything, but Leaf could almost hear *Again?* swirling around her head. The red pandas, who always ate whatever they found whenever they found it, without any kind of blessing or gathering, were still getting used to traveling with the pandas. Leaf didn't feel guilty—the Nine Feasts were important. They were how they showed the Great Dragon that they were still listening for its voice. Obviously the red pandas wouldn't understand, and that was okay.

They stopped for the Feast of Long Light at the top of a hill. On one side the hill fell away as a craggy cliff, and Leaf sat near the edge to eat her feast, looking down at the climb they'd already made. She gazed at the Slenderwood they had left behind, and at the glistening surface of the winding river.

Dasher came and sat beside her, and yawned hugely.

"It's weird, isn't it?" he said.

"Very," said Leaf. She crunched her bamboo thoughtfully. "I can't stop thinking about our names. I'm no longer Leaf Slenderwood. What will I be, when we get where we're going? Will I ever get used to being called . . . I don't know, Leaf Highslope? Or Greencrag? Or something? And what do I call myself *now*? While we're traveling I'm . . . I'm Leaf Nowhere."

"That's the good thing about our names," said Dasher, rolling over and stretching. "Could be anything you do. Or things you don't do, sometimes. You can invent your own, or join a new family, if you don't like the one you're born with. Hey, you could be Leaf Climbing Far! Although I think some of the red pandas think you should all be called Panda Stopping Often," he added, giggling, and Leaf laughed along with him until quiet fell between them once more.

"I always thought that if I ever left the Slenderwood, it would be to cross the river," she said eventually. "To go and be with my mother, and my twin. Now we're going in the opposite direction. I guess I'll never cross the river now."

"Never say never." Dasher sat up and turned to look to the north, and Leaf followed his gaze. The White Spine Mountains glittered in the distance, their snowy slopes just visible beyond the forested crags. "Do you think Plum made it to the top?"

"I hope so."

They walked on, stopping for more feasts as Long Light and Sun Fall pushed into Dying Light. The pandas began to talk of stopping for the night, finding somewhere that would feed them for Moon Climb, Moon Fall, and Gray Light before they moved on again. But bamboo was hard to find, and more than once the red pandas accidentally led them on a path with a dead end, meeting a solid wall of rock or a thicket so tangled they couldn't get through.

Dying Light itself was fading, and the air was growing cold and dark. Leaf walked slowly, waiting for word from Wanderer or one of the others. She saw that Cane was riding on

Hyacinth's back again, his little legs too weak for all this walking, and the other pandas' eyes were starting to droop too. They were picking their way along the side of a slope, and it was getting steeper, so it was hard work to keep their footing, each panda unbalanced, with one paw higher than the other.

Leaf was also becoming aware of more and more chatter among the red pandas, and not the normal gossip she would hear in the Slenderwood. There was a worried, whispery tone to their voices, except when one of them would snap at another and make all the pandas jump.

"I *know* it's dark!" Hunter said up ahead.

The red panda he'd been whispering with gave an unhappy growl. "Well, we have to stop soon," she told him. "Bamboo or not. We're *lost.*"

A chorus of worried noises went up from the pandas and the red pandas alike. Hunter spun to look at them, his tail lashing in the pine needles underfoot.

"We are not lost!"

"We are," put in Splasher. "We need to stop—we could be going in any direction now. We might have already doubled back on ourselves."

"You want to sleep right here, out in the open? We need to find bamboo and climbable trees."

"But how are we going to find them in the dark?" Hyacinth said, clambering closer to the bickering red pandas.

"By scent," Hunter snarled. "The same way the tiger's going to find *us!*"

A hush fell over the whole group, until it was broken by

the sound of Cane keening, a low, panicky sound. Hyacinth turned away to comfort her cub, and the red pandas fell back to arguing among themselves.

Leaf took a step back, trying to fight down the panic in her own heart. They would be okay. They would. The Great Dragon would help them. . . .

Then something caught her eye, moving between the trees. For a moment, she was too afraid to even cry out. It was dark, almost like a solid shadow, and it moved sinuously, like a snake—but it was too big to be a snake.

But it wasn't the tiger, either. She watched it, frozen with confusion. Whatever it was, it was coming closer and closer, faster and faster, leaving a trail of dislodged pine needles in its wake. It curled between the trees, passing so close to Leaf that, just for a moment, she saw that it had form after all—the dim moonlight gleamed on a pattern like scales.

In a flash, she saw more strange details: feet with clawed toes, a silky fin, a glimpse of fur.

Leaf's heart began to beat faster than she had ever known. Her fear was gone, and in its place there was a joy so sharp it made her want to cry out.

And then the shape had passed her. She spun around to follow it, but it had vanished, in a way nothing that size should be able to. There was no sign that anything had ever been there . . . except, no, there was still a trail, as if something large had dragged itself through the pine needles.

She began to follow the trail.

"Leaf," Dasher said, scampering to her side. "What are you

doing? Did you see the tiger?"

"I saw . . . something," Leaf said. She couldn't bring herself to say what it had been. Not yet. But if she was right . . .

"Everyone," Dasher called back. "Leaf's found something!"

Leaf thought the red pandas must be grateful for the distraction, because soon she found herself leading the whole group up the slope, following the trail that the black shape had left. It wound between the trees, nearly vertical at one point, up and over a sharp ridge. But then the ground suddenly evened out to a comfortable climb up a gentle slope. She followed the trail until she came out of the shadow of trees into an open space and saw up ahead a pair of tall, pale rocks, lit by moonlight. She headed for them and stepped through the gap in between, to find herself looking down the other side of the hill. There was a gentle slope, a copse of wide-branched and climbable trees, and even a small forest of bamboo, its green leaves waving in the chilly breeze.

"Leaf!" The red pandas ran up to her and nudged their heads against her affectionately, before scampering down the slope toward the trees.

"You found the way!" said Gale. She gave Leaf a big affectionate lick on the cheek. "However did you know?"

Leaf looked at Gale, and Gale's expression turned a little worried.

"Leaf, are you all right?"

"I saw a shape in the forest," she said slowly. "It was long, like a snake, but huge and black. It passed by me, almost as close as you are now. It showed me where to go."

There was a heavy, stunned silence.

"The Dragon," breathed Juniper.

"It showed us the way," Crabapple said, his eyes glistening with tears in the moonlight. "It's watching over us after all!"

"Perhaps Plum found its cave and woke it up?" Hyacinth wondered.

"Things will get better for us now," Juniper said. "You wait and see."

The pandas laughed and chattered over this thought as they ran down the slope and prepared themselves for the Feast of Moon Climb. But Leaf didn't follow them just yet. She stayed behind by herself, at the top of the hill between the tall rocks.

It wasn't that she wasn't as happy as the others. If anything, she felt happier than she ever had in her life. She felt as if she were glowing.

The breeze blew through the gap between the rocks, stirring her fur. But instead of the chilly mountain air, it was warm. She shivered with excitement as the breeze curled itself around her, and then it was gone.

The Great Dragon really was with them.

*The Great Dragon . . . is with* me.

# CHAPTER TWELVE

THE WIND BLEW COLD and hard across the frozen plain, coming in vicious bursts broken up by deceptive moments of calm. It carried no scent but that of ice and rock.

"How much longer should we—" Frost began, but the wind cut him off, crossing between the leopard cubs with a howl and forcing Frost to turn his head and squeeze his eyes closed against a shower of sleet.

Ghost hunkered down, trying to sniff at the ground, but he could smell nothing except the other cubs. His stomach rumbled, loud enough that the whistling wind didn't quite cover it.

The deer had been good, while it lasted. The cubs had been full, and content. But even a whole deer couldn't last a family of five leopards forever, and now it was all gone and they were hungry again. Ghost stared across the rocky, empty expanse.

*I'll never know what it's like not to go hungry between meals,* he thought. *I'll never be a good enough hunter for that....*

"Just a little longer," said Snowstorm. "The wind might've driven the prey underground. Focus on sniffing for burrows and dens."

"Ghost," said Shiver. "Have you tried it yet?"

Ghost sighed. He knew Shiver meant well. She wanted to remind the others of his triumph with the deer. But the problem was, he *had* tried asking the Snow Cat for help. He'd asked four times already that morning, and there had been no warm breath on his fur and no paw prints in the snow.

"The Snow Cat's not going to do *all* our hunting for us," Snowstorm told Shiver, before Ghost could answer.

"Anyway, maybe we really did just get lucky last time," Frost muttered.

"It was real," Ghost said. "I know it."

"Hmm," said Frost, and looked away to sniff at the ground.

Ghost closed his eyes and turned his face to the sky.

"Snow Cat, please show us your paw prints that we may follow them," he said, but in his heart he wanted to beg the Snow Cat for more than just prey. He wanted answers.

*Snow Cat, why would you help me before, and not now? Why would you make me feel useful, then show me that I'm not at all? If you have a purpose for me, if I have a place on this mountain, why do you always hide it from me?*

The Snow Cat didn't answer.

The cubs split up to search the ice field for burrowing creatures, but though Shiver found the scent of a hare, when they dug out the burrow, it was empty.

"Let's go," Frost yowled to the others eventually. "This isn't worth it."

Ghost nodded, and a few of the ice crystals that had attached themselves to the tips of his fur crumbled off. The cubs' tails were all crunchy with frost.

"Let's head for the trees," Snowstorm agreed. "It's more sheltered. Maybe there'll be prey there."

She led the way across the expanse of rock and snow toward a dark line of treetops at the edge of the ridge. As the cubs walked, the clouds ahead of them broke up, so that thin streams of sunlight began to sweep across the landscape, moving and changing with the swift flow of the clouds high overhead. The sun was warm, but so bright that when it caught the cubs head-on, it half blinded them, stopping them in their tracks just as surely as the blistering wind.

They climbed down a snowy slope to the edge of the small forest. Thin pine trees clung to the mountain, growing up between the cracks in the rocks. Each rough trunk branched into two or three spreading needle canopies at the top, casting dark zigzagging shadows over the ground as the bright shafts of sunlight passed over them.

"Walk as silently as you can," Snowstorm whispered, repeating Winter's advice. "The pine needles are crunchy, so keep to the rocks. And don't forget, the prey could be above us."

Ghost glanced up at the branches of the trees. He knew he could climb up, but what would he do when he got there? He couldn't pounce to save his life on a flat surface, so he certainly wasn't going to try it in a tree. . . .

Parts of the forest floor were flat stretches of soft earth under a thin carpet of snow and pine needles. In other places the trees grew right out from between shelves of rock that formed steps and ridges along the edge of the mountain.

Snowstorm, Frost, and even Shiver seemed to have no problem finding their way through the uneven landscape, bounding down drops twice as tall as they were, keeping balance with their tails, leaping from rock to tree branch and back.

Ghost watched silently as they started to draw away from him. He didn't bother calling out to them to wait. He wasn't sure he could go where they were going at all, let alone at their speed. He'd let them get on with it. It would be better for them all if one of them caught something. He wouldn't be bitter. He wouldn't let himself.

His heart was heavy, though, as he nosed around the rocks to find a way that was safe for him to go. The shafts of light cutting through the tree trunks made the patches of snow on the ground glow sparkling white, and Ghost found himself dazzled more than once, stopping not just to keep his balance, but to blink away the dancing afterimages.

He paused at the edge of a wide crack that sloped down between two rocks, sniffing around for prey. If he was very, very lucky, he might find a fat partridge sleeping in the warm shafts of sunlight, or maybe a completely deaf squirrel. . . .

But it wasn't the scent of living prey that he found. Instead he smelled something completely unfamiliar. It reminded him of earth, mulchy and wet like the lowest slopes of the mountain, and the smell of old blood. It was a predator smell, but it was definitely not a leopard.

*Something's here.* . . .

He pulled back, looking around for his siblings.

There was no sign of them.

"Shiver?" He called his littermate's name, but softly, hoping that she might be nearby after all. But there was no reply.

He turned and climbed up the nearest pine tree, his paws shaky on the rough trunk. Normally, climbing was one thing he could do as well and almost as quietly as his littermates, but anxiety made him hurry, and the tree branch bent and swayed underneath him as he pulled himself up onto it.

He still couldn't see them, though he squinted into the shafts of light and shadow for a long moment, looking for any movement against the snow. He paused, freezing as still as possible and sniffing the air for the familiar scents of fluff and of Winter's den, straining his ears for the sound of pine needles crackling under paws. . . .

Then a frightened yowl echoed between the rocks, and Ghost's heart dropped into the pit of his stomach. He slid from the branch and down the trunk in a controlled tumble, landing hard on his flank on the rock below. The sound had come from just over a ridge of rock in front of him. He clambered up as fast as he could, finding claw holds and pushing himself off the jutting trunks of trees, until at last he came to the top and looked down onto a wide shelf, circled with trees and carpeted with pine needles, where Shiver, Snowstorm, and Frost were all huddled with their backs to a sheer rock face.

Stalking closer to them, surrounding them and cutting off their escape, were three strange creatures. They had short, black fur, and they weren't like the leopards—for a start, they were bigger. On their chests they bore a bright orange circle, almost like a huge version of a leopard's spot.

They moved slowly, almost clumsily, but there was a power in their bunched muscles. Their faces were long, with pale orange muzzles that came to a point at a round nose, and no whiskers at all. They were snarling furiously at the three leopard cubs. One of them opened its jaws, and Ghost saw a long tongue curl out, tasting the air.

"Who trespasses on our resting place?" the largest of the three creatures snarled, in a voice like thunder rolling over the mountain. Now that he looked closer, one of the things was smaller than the other two—a cub? It was bigger than any of the leopards, though not very much bigger than Ghost himself. The other two were a male and a female, most likely the cub's parents.

He saw Snowstorm steel herself, her fur standing on end, and step forward with her tail raised defensively high.

"We are the cubs Born of Winter," she said bravely, keeping her voice steady. "And we didn't mean to interrupt your sleep."

"Leopards," said the large female, sniffing. "They can be

dangerous, but . . . these are such small ones. And I'm so hungry, Obsidian. . . ."

"Prey *is* scarce in this wretched frozen place," growled her mate. He took a step forward, and the three cubs instinctively pressed together. Snowstorm bared her teeth, but she was trembling, her eyes wide with terror.

Ghost let out a roar and leaped. He landed hard and awkwardly on the next rock down, and then the next, making as much noise as he could as he jumped from ledge to ledge.

"Get away from my littermates!" he snarled as he landed in the clearing, baring his teeth and snapping his powerful jaws at the three strange black creatures. All three of them spun, kicking up pine needles, and stared at him in anger and confusion.

"What is this?" Obsidian roared. "What are you?"

"I'm a cub Born of Winter too!" Ghost roared back. "And I'll snap your neck in my teeth if you hurt my littermates!"

Ghost had expected a fight. He'd expected the things to roar back, to flee if he was very lucky, and to kill him if he wasn't. He was already half turning to yell to the others to run, when he saw the aggressive stances of the black creatures soften. They looked at each other, and then at Ghost, as if he had said something deeply confusing instead of threatening to kill them. The cub even sat back on its haunches and tilted its head.

"But it's not a leopard. It's a bear," he said.

Ghost growled, but it was a weak, uncertain growl. "I'm no bear! What . . . what's a bear?"

"We are," said the female.

"Ghost's nothing like you!" Shiver mewed, then hopped back behind Snowstorm when the female bear turned her pointed muzzle to look at her.

"No, he's not one of us. We're sun bears. The Great Dragon made the mark of the sun on us, see?" said Obsidian. He raised a paw to his chest and scratched at the orange mark with his claws. Ghost noticed that even though he seemed more relaxed now, the claws didn't retract as he put them down.

"You're a friend to these cats, little bear?" asked the female.

"They're my littermates," Ghost said again. Why couldn't these bears understand that? He wasn't like them at all. . . .

"Well, if they're your . . . friends," the female said, and Ghost bristled at her choice of word, "then we'll spare them. You can all go."

"Did you come to live here after the flood too?" asked the cub. He padded a few steps toward Ghost, sniffing the air.

"Careful, Shale," said Obsidian, though he didn't try to stop him.

"The flood destroyed our forest," the cub went on. "That's why we're traveling through these mountains. Mother says it was warm there, and we ate fish, but I don't remember. Did you come from somewhere like that?"

Ghost couldn't really take in everything the bear cub was saying, but he shook his head.

"You're—you're all wrong. I come from here," he said miserably. "I'm Born of Winter, just like them."

"Then you must be some kind of snow bear," said the female

thoughtfully. "I wish you luck, whatever you are." She turned, calling her cub to her with a jerk of her head, and Shale ran to her side. The bears began to pad away, climbing up over the rocks. The leopard cubs started to slink toward Ghost, keeping a careful distance from the bears as they did so. Before they vanished between the trees, the bear called Obsidian turned and looked down at Ghost. His expression was kind, but puzzled.

"Shale is right, cub," he said. "You're no leopard."

And then he was gone over and down behind a rock shelf. The last thing Ghost saw was his stubby black tail.

"Well done, Ghost!" Snowstorm said, and rubbed her muzzle against his shoulder. "You saved us!"

Shiver bounced excitedly on the spot and jumped up over Ghost's back, before curling against his flank to catch her breath. "You were so brave!"

Ghost just stared at the place where the bears had been. He felt cold, colder even than when the wind on the plain had been frosting his fur with ice crystals.

"Why did they think I was one of them?" he asked in a small voice.

"That was so weird." Shiver gave Ghost's closest paw an affectionate lick.

"I—I'm not one of them, am I?"

"No way," said Frost. "There are no 'snow bears.'" But he had a thoughtful look on his face as he looked at Ghost's paws, and at his short tail, and it made Ghost's heart race with panic.

Ghost turned to Snowstorm. She would tell him the truth.

She was the one who always looked at both sides of things.

"Of course not," she said. She padded in front of him and sat down, giving him a lick on the top of his head just like Winter had done for them all when they were small. "Ghost, you're special—but you're still one of us. We all know you're Born of Winter, just like us. Where else could you have come from?"

They finally managed to scent and catch a couple of hares on the plains. They had come out of their burrows when the wind calmed and the bright sunlight warmed the air, and they made a good meal for the cubs Born of Winter before they headed home to the den.

As they walked down the slope, picking their way over rocks and down snowy banks, they passed by a rock face that was covered in ice. The sleet had added another layer of frost, and the sunshine had melted it so that the surface was slick and reflective.

The movement of Ghost's reflection caught his eye and he looked. Then he stopped.

His littermates padded on, cheerful from their narrow escape and full bellies, and he let them walk ahead before he approached the ice and looked more closely at his own features.

He was larger and broader than a leopard should be. His muzzle was longer, his nose larger and rounder. His paws weren't the same shape. His claws didn't retract. His tail was short. His fur was thin, his head and ears were round, his legs were short . . .

Ghost began to shake as he sat there, alone on the side of the mountain, looking at his reflection and seeing, now that he had a name for it, a bear.

*What is that? What am I?*

A roar of agony built up in his chest, but he couldn't let it out. The other cubs—the *real* cubs—would hear him, and would come back, and he couldn't face them now. He reared up and clawed at the ice, but he couldn't make it break away from the rock. All he did was leave jagged scratches across the surface, and even those melted away as he watched.

*What am I?*

Not a leopard. It was bitterly, *comically* obvious. He wondered how he had managed to convince himself he was a leopard all this time.

*Winter lied to me.*

A red flush of hate bubbled up inside him, new and raw and terrifying.

*She lied! She let me think I was a broken, freakish leopard, when I'm something else completely! I'm not her cub. And I don't belong here, just like Brisk and Sleet always said.*

Ghost sank to the ground, still shaking, and curled up with his paws over his eyes, as if hiding from his reflection would make it not true.

*Then where did I come from? Who is my real mother, if not Winter?*

*Who am I?*

# CHAPTER THIRTEEN

SUNSET SAT UP IN the crook of a tree at the edge of the feast clearing, his eyes shut, his little blue stone held lightly in one paw. The Prosperhill pandas gathered around the base of the tree, staring up at him. Peony bent down and let Maple climb on her back so he could see better.

Rain sat at the edge of the group, watching as intently as the others—well, perhaps not as intently as Pebble, who was sitting right below the tree and practically holding his breath. Rain knew they were watching for very different things. Pebble's expression was full of wonder. He believed that Sunset would open his eyes and share with them all the thoughts of the Great Dragon, a wise and ancient being.

Rain expected Sunset to lie.

She didn't know what the lie was going to be, or what he was going to get out of it, but she knew that it would be a lie, and that she was the only one who wouldn't believe it.

There were more pandas in the feast clearing than ever before, but Rain had never felt quite so alone.

Sunset raised the Seeing Stone higher and higher, so high that there was an intake of breath from the pandas as they thought he might lose his balance and topple from the branch. But Sunset knew what he was doing, and he lowered the stone again slowly and then climbed down the tree, still with his eyes firmly shut. When he stood on the ground again, he opened his eyes with a gasp.

*You're laying it on a bit thick now,* Rain thought. Surely some other panda would start to think it was all a bit ridiculous too? What about the fact that he hadn't done any of this performance last time?

But every other Prosperhill panda seemed completely focused on the Dragon Speaker, waiting anxiously for him begin.

"The Dragon has spoken to me," Sunset proclaimed. "The words are these: *A breeze will carry the scents of summer through the Bamboo Kingdom.*"

"Oooh," said several of the pandas.

"What does that mean?" whispered Frog.

"It could mean lots of things," Dawn whispered back.

*It means the seasons will change and the wind will blow,* Rain thought. *It means he's just saying things that he knows will definitely happen so they don't know he's a faker.*

*It means I'm right.*

A thrill of vindication that felt like a shudder ran under her fur.

Sunset accepted an armful of fresh bamboo from Pebble, and slumped down to eat it as if climbing a tree and waving a rock around had been deeply exhausting. The other pandas went back to their feasts too, speculating about the Dragon's message.

"It means good times are coming," proclaimed Bay. "It'll be warmer soon."

"The part about scent must mean something too," said Pebble. He sat down near Rain, but he didn't look at her, talking to Bay and Dawn. "Maybe there'll be a new scent, and when we all smell it we'll know some change is coming."

"Or maybe summer won't come here at all," said Crag, settling down near them. "The Dragon was always keen on warnings. Maybe it's saying the best bamboo this year will grow elsewhere, and we'll have to use our noses to find it."

*Oh, come on!* Rain almost interrupted them. How could they find so much to say about such an empty message? But she knew that if she said something, she'd risk tipping off Sunset that she knew he was full of nonsense—and also, Pebble was nodding along to Crag's stupid theory, crunching his bamboo with a thoughtful frown on his face.

It hurt her heart to let her best friend go on not knowing he was being lied to, but she knew that she still had no proof strong enough to convince him. If she tried to tell him, they'd only argue again, and she couldn't bear that.

She decided she couldn't stay here and listen to any more of this. Soon they would decide that the message meant that the sky was green and the river would run backward. She got up to leave, but before she could get out of the feast clearing, she heard her name called and turned to see Sunset trotting after her.

"Rain," he said. "I wanted to ask, have you made any progress with the river?"

Rain bristled, but tried to hide her annoyance. Even if she'd been searching as hard as she could, surely it would be many feasts before she found a crossing place no Prosperhill panda had ever found before.

"Well . . ." She sat down and scratched her neck with one long claw. "I've been looking into it. There are some places where the current's stronger than in others, but the shallows can be deceptively calm. You can tell—if you're an experienced swimmer, I mean—when you're getting into water that's dangerous, and sometimes it's just a paw-length farther from the shore. I haven't found a spot where the middle's running calm enough to cross, yet."

"Well, that's still good progress," Sunset said, and gave her a friendly grin. Rain suppressed the urge to scowl back at him.

"Thanks," she said. "I'm glad to help."

*See?* she thought. *I can lie too. And more convincingly than you can.*

"Keep looking," said Sunset. "And may the Great Dragon guide you."

Rain nodded, and headed out of the clearing to pretend to go to the river, but a slight chill passed over her as she thought again about her dream. It had been so vivid, so *specific*. She could almost feel the spray from the waterfall tickling her nose even now. She'd never heard anyone talk about the Dragon having three heads, so why would she have dreamed that up?

She shook herself. She was acting just like the others, trying to drag meaning into things that meant nothing. She needed proof of Sunset's lies, and she wasn't going to get it if she didn't *do* something.

A few paces from the clearing, when she was sure that there was no way Sunset could possibly see her, she hid underneath a large, spreading bush and waited, listening intently. She heard the other pandas begin to leave the clearing too, some of them talking, some still munching on the last of their feasts. An unfamiliar scent passed by; then she realized it was Maple, his high voice chattering to Peony as they walked. Rain's heart warmed to see the two of them sticking together. Her mother would protect him. She wouldn't let Sunset or the monkeys do anything to hurt him.

Finally, she scented Sunset coming closer. She held her breath and kept perfectly still as he padded past. She let him vanish almost completely from sight before she moved, creeping to the next bush, and then a rock, and then the trunk of a large tree, following the Dragon Speaker through the forest.

Where would he go? Would he behave like a normal panda and lie down to sun himself on a rock, or have a between-feasts snack, or just go for a walk up and down the rolling crags? Or was there something else he had planned for this Long Light?

A couple of times she thought he had scented or heard her following him, and she had to press herself into the undergrowth and wait to find out if he would change his course. But although he looked around once or twice, he seemed to be convinced that he was alone, and he carried on walking in the same direction.

*This isn't just a Long Light wander. He's headed somewhere,* Rain thought as she peered carefully around the side of a rock to see Sunset padding straight across a trickling stream, his paws splashing in the cool, clear water.

She followed, treading slowly so as not to let the water make too much noise as she crossed the stream after him.

Finally she reached the crest of a hill and saw, down below her, a large rock under a big, twisted pine tree. Brawnshanks the golden monkey was sitting on it, picking at his fur with his strange long fingers. He looked up toward Sunset as the Dragon Speaker approached him, and Rain quickly hunkered down in a thicket of tall ferns to watch what would happen.

"Good Long Light, O good and wise Dragon Speaker," said Brawnshanks, and then gave a chittering laugh that was echoed by the troop of monkeys that lazed along the branches of the tree above him. A few of them swung down onto the ground around Brawnshanks's rock.

"Thank you, friend," said Sunset, although his voice was cool. "Where is it, then?"

"Oh, close by, close by," said Brawnshanks. "What's your rush, clever one?"

Sunset roared. The sound made Rain jump, and the ferns

all around her bounced and shook. She had never heard him roar like that. The monkeys jumped too, and a few of the ones on the rock fell off, or leaped reflexively back up into the tree, but they giggled as they went. Brawnshanks scratched himself calmly under the chin.

"Don't test me, monkey," Sunset growled. "We have a deal, remember? I have a lot more prophecies to make, and it isn't working. I need more dream leaf *now*."

"So far, as I see it, this deal has mostly benefited you," said Brawnshanks thoughtfully. Sunset took a threatening step toward his rock. "Don't worry," the monkey added, still not moving a muscle, although several of his troop hopped away to keep their distance from the Dragon Speaker. "It really is close by. You sit right here, and we'll be back with your precious dream leaf." He patted the rock, giggled again, and then sprang into the trees. The monkey troop took off, whooping and bouncing along the branches and away. Sunset sat down with his back against a tree and huffed in annoyance.

Rain made a decision.

She carefully, quietly extracted herself from the ferns, and then turned and ran, as stealthily as she could, after the monkeys.

It was much more of a chase than she'd had with Sunset. The monkeys moved fast, and sometimes apparently at random, so she would be running from one hiding spot to the next when the whole troop took a sharp turn, leaping from one tree to another, and she had to skid to a halt and plunge into the undergrowth to keep herself hidden.

*It's not all that close,* she thought as she peered through the branches. *Sunset may be a liar, but it seems he's also being lied to.* . . .

They were much too quick for her to keep up for long, but luckily, they made such a racket as they went that she could easily follow the sound. If that failed, she could scent around for leaves that had recently dropped from the trees and find the ones that carried the strongest monkey smell—sickly sweet from their diet of fruit, flowers, and insects.

She ran on until the sounds grew louder again, and then louder still. She heard the monkeys shouting to each other, somewhere high above her head, and then the trees parted and she found herself at the bottom of a wide space between two large, nearly sheer cliffs, looking up at one of the huge standing columns of rock that sometimes stuck up by themselves between the hills of the Southern Forest. It was covered in moss, vines, and ferns that had managed to cling to the cracks in the rock, and at the top there was a small, wavering clump of bamboo with striped canes and leaves. The whole column looked like a hulking creature, rearing up with its fur standing on end.

The monkeys were swarming up the rock, grabbing the vines and jumping from ledge to ledge. Rain could just make out which one was Brawnshanks—he was a little larger than the rest, and he moved with more purpose, while the rest of the troop swung wildly and excitably around him. He scrambled to the top of the rock and waited for the rest of his troop to catch up and settle near him before pointing at the bamboo, giving out orders in his chattering voice, which Rain had to strain to hear.

". . . every monkey grab a handful. Nimbletail, you get up there to the top."

The monkeys began to climb the bamboo trunks, reaching the sprays of leaves and tugging to pull them free. The monkey Brawnshanks had called Nimbletail, one of the smallest, climbed right to the top of one. She clung to the stalk as it wavered back and forth, and plucked the leaves from the very end. Rain's stomach clenched instinctively as the young monkey dangled over the long drop down to the forest floor, but the terrifying height and wild bouncing movement clearly didn't bother Nimbletail one bit. Rain had to admit, these creatures had nerves as strong as the trunk of a gingko tree. Soon the monkeys were clambering back down with big bunches of stripy bamboo leaves clenched in their hands and in their teeth.

Rain kept still and quiet as they swung back past her, presumably to deliver the bamboo—the dream leaf—to Sunset.

Rain didn't need to see the handover. There was something else she wanted to do.

When the sound of the monkeys had died away completely, she emerged from her hiding place and approached the column of rock. She swallowed as she looked up at it. It was taller than the tallest tree she had ever climbed, and she was no monkey.

But the striped bamboo only seemed to grow up there.

She circled the rock, looking carefully at its cracks and crevices before she decided which side would be easiest to start climbing. She picked out a route that looked like it had plenty of claw holds and began, slowly, to pull herself up.

She wasn't, she reluctantly admitted to herself as she reached from ledge to ledge, the strongest climber in the Prosperhill. She forced herself to take it slowly, and reminded herself not to trust the vines—they were tempting to grab on to, but while they might hold the weight of the monkeys for a few moments, a whole panda was a different thing entirely. She tried not to look down, but she couldn't help stealing glances between her paws. She looked back after a while, and it seemed like all at once she had made it almost to the top of the tree canopy. The emptiness of the air around her almost seemed to tug on her. She focused quickly on the rock in front of her nose, and tried to pretend that the ground was still just beneath her back paws. . . .

She was nearing the top when her paw slipped on a patch of wet moss and she scrambled, howling with terror, managing to dig her front claws deep into a crack between the rocks while she found her footing again. She stayed quite still for a while after that, clinging on to the side of the column until she felt herself stop shaking.

Finally, she pulled herself up and over onto the flattish top of the rock, and lay flopped there until she had caught her breath, closing her eyes so she could pretend she was just lying on a nice low rock ledge on the side of a hill somewhere.

Then she sat up and carefully shifted so she could look out from the top of the rock without losing her balance. The view was amazing, out over the thick canopy of green and gold, the two steep cliffs on either side framing a view of more hills rising in the distance, bright and lush in the strong sunlight. She glanced down and then pulled back sharply as the ground seemed to waver beneath her, like the bottom of the river on a clear day.

Getting back down was going to be a challenge.

But before that, she had to find out what was so special about this bamboo. Sitting on the mossy top of the rock, she was nose to nose with the small cluster of bamboo stalks, with their strange stripy leaves. She sniffed them carefully. They smelled like bamboo—woody and fresh, perhaps slightly tangier than normal.

Sunset had called this dream leaf. So it had to give him visions, visions he could use to fake the Dragon's messages. She picked a pawful of leaves and eyed them suspiciously. She needed to be sure. But what if she ate them, was transported into another weird dream like the one she'd had by the river, and fell off the column of rock and smashed her head?

*Just get on with it!*

Rain made sure she was firmly, securely settled on the top of the rock. Then, very carefully, she nibbled on the end of the bunch of leaves.

"Blech!" She stuck her tongue out and licked at her own fur, trying to scrape off the chewed-up plant bits. They were incredibly, disgustingly bitter. "Ugh, blech!" She shook her head and smacked her jaws.

"Well, he's definitely not eating this for the taste," she muttered.

Sunset had said he needed lots of it. With a shudder, she stuffed the whole bunch into her mouth and chewed hard. Bitter plant juices ran over her tongue and she winced, but she kept on chewing and forced herself to swallow. Then she sat back and waited.

Nothing seemed to happen immediately. Rain leaned against the thick, bending trunks of the bamboo.

*Come on, dreams,* she thought, *I'm ready for you. Whatever this stuff is for, I'm ready to find out.*

She swallowed another horrible bunch, then another to make sure. But still nothing happened.

She waited for a long time on top of the rock, as Long Light turned into Sun Fall. She didn't want to start the long, scary climb back down the rock until she was sure she wouldn't suddenly start seeing dragons on the way down. But finally it looked like no visions or dreams were coming, so she set off, feeling her way carefully backward down the side of the column. By the time she reached the bottom, she still felt nothing unusual of any kind, except for the lingering bitter taste on her tongue.

She started back for the feast clearing with a thoughtful growl in her chest.

*Sunset thinks he'll get visions if he eats enough of that stuff.*

*But it hasn't worked for me. So probably it won't work for him. Are the monkeys fooling him into eating those revolting leaves? But why?*

Of one thing Rain was certain: If Sunset thought he needed help making his prophecies, he was no Dragon Speaker. He was nothing of the kind.

# CHAPTER FOURTEEN

LEAF WALKED AT THE front of the pandas as they continued their winding journey up through the foothills of the White Spine Mountains, with Dasher at her side and the other red pandas circling as they had the day before, sometimes running ahead and sometimes falling behind, always watching for any sign of the tiger.

The Dragon hadn't returned, but the trail it had left led them to a clear and obvious path that wound between the peaks of the hills and up, always up, toward the mountains. Leaf didn't really need to be the one to lead the way—the path was clear to all the pandas—but the others had insisted that since she'd seen the Dragon, obviously she should go first, in case it came back.

After the Feast of Sun Climb they were walking along a high ridge when Leaf and Dasher came out of the slanting shade of the trees onto a bare open space, and suddenly caught up with a group of red pandas who had been scouting ahead.

"What's the matter? Did you smell something?" Leaf asked.

"Look," said Jumper, who was among them. Leaf looked, and saw what had caused them to stop. All at once, up on this ridge, they had a clear view of the mountains to the north. The White Spine with its long, icy plains and sharp crevasses, and beyond that, in the direction of the sunrise, the Dragon Mountain. It loomed jagged and purple against the morning sky, its summit vanishing into clouds that seemed to curl around it, clinging to its sharp sides.

"That's where the Dragon's cave is," Leaf breathed. "They say that the cloud around it is the dragon's breath."

"Well, that looks . . . inviting," said Dasher. "Perfectly safe and not at all like somewhere we might freeze to death."

"It's okay," Leaf said. She understood why the mountain made the red pandas jumpy, but she felt perfectly calm. "The Dragon wants us to go there. We'll be okay."

"It wants *you* to go there," muttered Chomper.

"Come on," Leaf said. "The path goes this way."

She pressed on, not minding that the wind was chilly up on the exposed ridge, or that the Dragon Mountain was still so far away. Perhaps they would find Plum soon. Perhaps she was already coming back from the Dragon's cave with good news.

The path led down from the ridge and up the side of the next hill, and through the middle of a patch of thorny bushes. Leaf wondered just what creatures had first made this path—something must travel this way, often. Perhaps it was the strange gray goats with the huge curling horns that they'd glimpsed grazing on the sides of the slopes.

As she was leading the other pandas through the thin gap between two thornbushes, Leaf spotted something white caught on one of the twigs. It was fur. She hurried toward it and carefully sniffed around the bush, and her heart swelled.

*Aunt Plum!*

"Plum has been here!" she turned to call back to the others.

"By the Nine Feasts," sighed Crabapple. "Thank the Dragon for that."

They emerged from the thornbushes and headed along the path as it wound between a few pine trees, talking about Plum's mission.

"I'm sure we'll find her soon," Leaf said, "If we just—"

"Tiger!"

Leaf broke off as Wanderer and Chomper came racing down the slope toward them. The pandas all stopped in their tracks and muttered to each other.

"The tiger's nearby," Chomper gasped. "The scent's getting stronger."

"It's following us," Wanderer said.

"Are you sure?" Leaf asked.

Wanderer looked at her darkly. "I know that scent. This thing is clever. It's been following us for a while, but stayed far away so we wouldn't smell it. Until we got lucky."

"What are we going to do?" Grass asked. "Should we run?"

"We shouldn't have come so far," Hunter muttered. "There's no food here and there's *still* a tiger."

"Or should we . . . should we try to face it?" Hyacinth wondered.

"We can't just let it follow us all the way to the Dragon Mountain," said Seeker.

"But we—"

Dasher was interrupted by a roar so loud, several pandas fell to the ground and pressed their paws over their ears. It trembled through the air around them, echoing off the sides of the hills. It sounded like an animal as big as the whole mountain opening its jaws and howling.

"The tiger!" shrieked Racer Climbing Far, and she turned tail and scampered back down the slope.

*Not even the tiger could make a sound that loud,* Leaf thought.

"Run!" said Grass, turning to follow her. One after another, the pandas and red pandas broke into a panicky, tumbling dash. Hyacinth seized Cane by the scruff of his neck and carried him.

"No, wait! Please, wait a moment!" Leaf tried to step in front of Wanderer, but he just ran between her legs and followed the others down through the bushes. They left the path and started to scramble down the slope. "I don't think that's the tiger! This isn't right—the Dragon showed us the way!" Leaf yelled after them. She spun to look for her best friend. "Dasher, please . . ."

"I'm with you," Dasher said, stepping close to Leaf and pressing himself to her side, his tail wrapping around her back leg and his ears pressed to his skull in terror. "But what was that? What do we do?"

"Grass! Seeker, Juniper! Please come back!" Leaf roared. But the other pandas weren't listening.

Then the world twisted underneath Leaf's paws. With a roar, the ground shook and began to rise up, lifting her and Dasher, and all the bushes and the trees. The earth cracked, rocks splintering into pieces. Leaf reached out and clamped her claws into the trunk of one of the closest pines as the ground crashed back, trembling and breaking up all around her, cleaving the rocks and sending up clouds of dust. One of the other trees tipped over and began to topple down the slope. Leaf saw it begin to roll, crashing down toward the other pandas.

"Watch out!" she yelled, but she could barely hear her own roar over the breaking of the earth. A great chunk of rock dislodged itself from the slope above her, and slithered downward. Dasher lost his footing and was dragged away from Leaf, scrabbling at the ground to try to climb the flowing earth beneath his paws. Leaf reached for him, and he managed to grab on to one of her claws, leaving them dangling by only one paw from the quivering tree.

Leaf looked down and saw the pandas and red pandas scattering out of the way of the rock, but they slipped and tumbled, trying and failing to grab on to bushes and rocks as they went. A cloud of dust exploded from a crack in the ground, obscuring most of her fellow pandas, though she could still hear their cries of panic.

The tree in her paw gave a horrible lurch.

"Up! We've got to go up!" Leaf yelled to Dasher. He

managed to climb up and over her, using her fur as a paw hold, and finally she pushed off from the tree just in time as it toppled forward, roots snapping and whipping out into the air as it hurtled down the slope.

Leaf dug her claws into the ground and climbed, ducking her head to keep from being blinded by the flood of dust and pebbles. The ground was still shaking and roaring like a terrified animal. She couldn't hear the other pandas anymore. But there was nothing else she could do. She just climbed. Dasher climbed beside her, his smaller paws less steady on the terrible slope.

"Leaf!" he gasped suddenly, and she looked up too late as a piece of bamboo tumbled into them. She braced herself, and its leaves brushed harmlessly against her, but the thicker part of the cane hit Dasher and he got tangled in the whipping branches. He lost his footing and began to fall.

"No!" Leaf barked, and turned around, letting go of her grip on the slope. As he fell, she launched herself down toward him and made a grab for his long striped tail with her jaws. She felt him jerk against her teeth and yell in pain, and she dug her claws into the earth again to stop herself from sliding face-first into the devastation below. The bamboo whipped on down the mountain, leaving Dasher behind.

Leaf turned, slowly, dragging Dasher with her. At last she saw a rock so large that it wasn't moving beyond a slow tremble, a still point in the river of earth. She made for it, and she and Dasher curled up together against its hard, solid surface and waited. They were close to the ridge of this hill, and little was left above them that could fall down, but now Leaf could see the other peaks, parts of them crumbling away, trees and rocks tumbling down to the bottom of the valleys. Flocks of birds had taken to the air and were circling, squawking in fear and confusion.

After a long while, the roaring of the earth grew quiet, and the shaking stopped altogether. There was a sound of creaking, as if the ground were letting out a long sigh, and then silence.

Leaf stepped gingerly out onto the slope and looked down. The dust was settling, but all she could see below her were crumbled rocks, fallen trees, and piles of dislodged earth.

There was no sign of the Slenderwood pandas or any of the red pandas.

She sat back, her paws shaking harder than they had during the long climb.

*We're all alone.*

# CHAPTER FIFTEEN

THE WIND THROUGH THE Endless Maw seemed to roar at Ghost as he stood on the edge of the crevasse, staring down into its depths. He wanted to roar back.

*What am I?*

The bottom of the Maw was barely visible, just a blurred line where the snow collected between the gray rocks. If he fell, he would hit the bottom so hard he might not even feel it—just a cold impact, and then nothing. That was if he didn't break every bone against the jagged sides of the crevasse on the way down.

He knew this. He knew the shape of his death, so clearly he could almost see the white figure sprawled in the darkness below.

But what else could he possibly do?

He had to know. Was he a leopard, or a bear? Was he Winter's cub at all? Where did he belong?

"I belong here!" He howled it into the wind with all his might, and the wind whipped it away like the last leaf from a bare tree. Ghost sank onto his belly in the snow and hung his head, trembling as he tried to catch his breath. "This is my home," he whispered. "And I can prove it."

He forced himself to look up, to fix his gaze on the column in the middle of the crevasse.

If he could make it across the Maw, that would settle it, forever. He could go back to believing that Winter was his mother. He could live in the snow-covered lands that were all he'd ever known.

*That's all I want,* Ghost thought, pressing his large paws down into the snow, feeling the prickling cold against his pads, the wetness getting under his freakish, non-retracting claws. *I just want things to go back to normal.*

If he made the jump, Icebound and her cubs would have to accept it, and so would his littermates. What's more, *Ghost* would have to accept it.

And if he couldn't make it across, then his bones would lie at the bottom of the Maw for all time, and he would never leave the White Spine Mountains.

*I don't want to die.*

He stood up and shook himself. He felt strength flowing through his limbs, and snapped his powerful jaws at the snow as it swirled past him.

*Then don't die!*

He ran, paws pounding on the snow, his heart high in his throat.

For one moment, he felt himself hesitate. It wasn't too late to turn back.

He forced himself to speed up, pushed past the point of no return with a defiant roar, felt the edge of the crevasse under his front paws, and leaped, reaching out for the column. He hung suspended in the air, the rock coming toward him . . .

But not fast enough.

Gravity seemed to reach up and snatch him from the air in its jaws, dragging him down into shadow. Ghost howled in fear as he tumbled into the darkness. Then, shockingly fast, he struck something. It bent and dipped under him. He scrambled with his claws and his teeth to grab hold of it. He failed, but the thing—a straggly tree branch—had broken his fall, and he managed to cling to it as he slid downward, until he landed, painfully, on a hard shelf of rock.

Ghost dug his claws into the soft wood of the tree trunk and pressed himself to the wall, squeezing his eyes shut and wheezing with terror, until he was sure that he truly wasn't falling anymore.

He finally opened his eyes and slowly, carefully, looked around him.

The tree was little more than one leafless branch, growing out of the wall of the crevasse. He hadn't even noticed it from up above.

*If I had made it even halfway to the column, I would have sailed over it and plummeted to my death.*

The shelf he was sitting on was a little wider than he was, and perhaps twice as long, jutting out from the side of the crevasse. It was covered in ice, and as he tried to let go of the tree and turn to look down, one of his paws slipped. Thank the Snow Cat, the rock sloped slightly toward the wall, so he just banged his shoulder against rock instead of tumbling farther into the depths.

The wall above him was nearly vertical, and the drop below was sheer, and still far enough that he knew he would break every bone in his body on the way down.

There was no way back.

Grief and shame and terror swirled around his head like the scattering snow blowing through the Maw.

He would die here, alone, in the darkness. Winter and the others would wonder what had happened to him, but they would probably never know. Perhaps they would think he'd left the mountains. He hoped they would.

He closed his eyes and pressed himself against the wall.

*Snow Cat, don't hurt them. Cover my body with snow and let Winter think that I found another life. A happy life . . .*

"Ghost!" yowled a terrified voice from the top of the Maw. Ghost jumped, his paws slipping again on the icy shelf, and looked up.

Four faces peered down over the edge, outlined against the cloudy sky. Shiver, Snowstorm, Frost, and Winter.

It was Shiver who had called to him. She edged closer to the drop, dangerously close, and Snowstorm had to put out a paw to stop her.

"Ghost, are you alive? Please be alive!" Shiver mewed.

"I saw him jump," Frost said, his voice shaking. "I couldn't get there in time to stop him. What do we do?"

"I'm here," Ghost said faintly. "I . . . I don't think I can get back." *Snow Cat, why? I asked you not to do this to them.*

"I'm coming, Ghost," Winter said. "I'll get you. You're going to be all right."

Ghost's heart thumped as he watched the shape of his mother pacing back and forth at the top of the crevasse, and then stepping down onto a tiny crack in the rock that Ghost hadn't even seen. Could she really do this?

*She's Winter. She can do anything.*

Ghost clung to the wall of the Maw and watched, unable to take his eyes off his mother as slowly, carefully, she made her way from ledge to ledge. Her tail whipped and tensed as she used it to balance herself on shelves of ice no wider than her paw, and with every step she paused and raked her claws through the ice, leaving a trail of white marks behind her, like the claws of the Snow Cat. She reared up to scratch across one ledge and wobbled on her perch as a gust of wind blew through her fur.

Ghost felt the shock of fear as if the Snow Cat itself had sunk its freezing fangs into his chest. "Don't fall," he mumbled aloud. "Oh please, please don't fall!"

If Winter heard him, she didn't reply. She found her balance and sought out the next ledge. Now she was just above Ghost's ledge, and she hopped down to join him on it with graceful ease, as if they were just practicing on the Training Rocks, safe on the even ground of the snowfield.

"Mother!" Ghost felt a surge of love for Winter and pulled himself along the ledge to press his forehead to hers. She licked the top of his head and his freezing face, and wrapped her long, thick tail around his trembling body.

"My boy," she rumbled. "My poor sweet boy. Thank the Snow Cat you're safe. But *why?* Why did you do it?"

Ghost pulled away and looked up into his mother's eyes—those eyes that were so familiar and full of love, but nothing at all like his own. His heart felt so heavy he was afraid the shelf beneath them would crack and fall away, but he knew he had to speak.

"Why—why did you tell me I was your cub?" He could feel his muzzle trembling as he forced the words out. "You're not my real mother. I'm not a leopard. Why did you let me believe I was?"

"Oh, Ghost." Winter's eyes swam with emotion. "Because I love you. I love you so much. You're my son, and you always will be, even if I didn't give birth to you."

Ghost knew it was true, had known since the bears—since before then, perhaps—but hearing it come from Winter herself was different. Pain and relief mingled together in his heart, like pulling a splinter of ice from a wound.

"Please tell me the truth," Ghost said. "What am I? Where did I come from?"

"I found you when you were very tiny." Winter sighed. "I heard mewling from inside a cave and I found you there, all alone. You were *so small*, and you had so little fur, you would have died if I hadn't found you—and so would I. While I was in the cave, an avalanche fell outside. You saved my life, Ghost. The Snow Cat sent you to me."

"And my—my mother?" Ghost asked.

Winter shook her head sadly. "I never saw her. I didn't know exactly what you were, at the time; I had never seen anything like you. But I knew that I had to protect you. When it was safe, I took you out of the cave and nursed you with your—with my cubs."

"I'm a bear," Ghost said miserably.

"I know," whispered Winter. "As you grew, I started to realize it. But I didn't want you to feel . . ."

"Different?" Ghost put in, with a slight snarl that he instantly regretted. Winter winced. But he had to go on. He had to make her understand. "You didn't want me to feel different, so you let me feel like a *failure*. I've always thought I was just a . . . a terrible leopard. I can't jump, can't hunt, not like the others. I've been struggling to keep up my whole life. *Different* would have been better."

"I see that now," Winter mewed. She dipped her head to her paws. "I'm so sorry, my cub."

"I don't belong here," Ghost said.

"You belong with me," Winter retorted. "With your family. We're—"

Then the ground seemed to slip out from under Ghost's

paws. He slid and fell to his belly on the ice shelf. But it hadn't cracked. It wasn't just the shelf; it was the entire Maw that was shaking and juddering.

Winter hunkered down, pressing herself close to him as small avalanches of snow poured down from the edge of the crevasse. Ghost dug his claws into the ice and waited for the shaking to stop, but it didn't. A roaring, cracking sound, so loud he couldn't think, echoed through the Endless Maw all around them. Winter looked up, her eyes full of fear, and Ghost knew she was worried there would be an avalanche. If the snow from the high peaks rolled over the crevasse, the cubs Born of Winter would be swept away, and she and Ghost would be crushed.

She pushed herself up and butted Ghost in the shoulder, even while the shelf beneath them was still shaking.

"Go!" Winter yowled over the roaring sound. "Follow my claw marks—you'll be able to climb up."

"I don't know if —"

"You can do it. *Listen to me.*" Winter leaned her forehead against Ghost's. "You're a great climber. You're strong. And that has nothing to do with being a leopard; it's about being *you*. I know you can make it. Now go! *Now!*" She put her paws on Ghost's shoulders and climbed over him, letting him past to get to the next ledge up. Ghost saw the claw marks and shuddered. He didn't have the balance of a leopard, or a tail. How could he ever make it up that steep climb, even if it wasn't trembling under his paws?

But he had no choice.

He reared up onto his hind legs, scrabbling for the first paw hold, and managed to hook his claws over the stone ledge. They vibrated almost painfully, but he clung on and pulled himself up.

*One down.*

He tried to look back at Winter, but the juddering rock made turning impossible.

"Don't look down," he heard her voice call up after him. "I'm right here. Just keep going."

Ghost tried to take a deep breath. He looked up and saw the three silhouettes of his littermates looking down from the edge of the Maw. Then he fixed his eyes on the next claw mark. It was only a few paw steps away, but the ledge it marked was tiny. He shuffled over, realizing what Winter meant—he had to hook his paw on to it and pull himself up, using it as a stepping-stone to the next, bigger ledge.

As he found a paw hold on the next crack, and the next, his heart was pounding with terror, but with something else, too.

*I can do this. Winter was right.*

He stopped to catch his breath on a wider shelf, just large enough to stand on with all four paws. There wasn't far to go now.

*I could have died down there without ever knowing I could climb out. But now, I actually might live.*

*I want to live!*

Another tremor roared through the ground, and Ghost heard Shiver's voice from above screaming, "Ghost, look out!" His head snapped up just in time to see a boulder, shaken loose from above, crashing down toward his ledge. He leaped for the next one, his back paws slipping on the icy rock. One of his front paws slid right off the ledge, and he dug his claws in as hard as he could with the other. The boulder slammed into the ledge, cracking it in two. Ghost dangled for a moment, scrabbling with his back legs on the rock wall, before finally pulling himself up to the next paw hold. He hung on, shaking, looking down at the broken shelf.

*That would have been my head.* The thought and the leap made him dizzy, and he squeezed his eyes shut for a second, but he knew he couldn't stop.

"You're nearly there, Ghost," said Snowstorm. There was fear in her voice, but he could hear that she was keeping her tone as calm as she could. She suddenly sounded just like Winter. "Just keep climbing."

"Hurry, Mother!" yelled Frost. "You can do it!"

They were only a few paw-lengths over his head. He was so tired, but he knew he could make it. Winter had shown him that he could.

Ghost tensed every muscle in his back as he dragged himself up and up, following one claw mark, then another . . . and then, finally, his paw slapped down into snow, and he felt the teeth of his littermates grabbing on to the fur at his neck. They dragged him up and over onto the flat, snowy plain.

"Good boy, Ghost!" he heard his mother's voice call from down below, and though he wanted to lie down on the still-shaking ground and never move again, he forced himself to get up so he could look over the edge.

Winter was still making her way behind him, only a few ledges back. She reached the ledge that had been cracked by the rock and tested it with her paw.

"Be careful, Mother!" Shiver yowled.

"It's all right," Winter called back. "I think it'll hold—"

But before she could put any weight on the ledge, there was a screaming sound of rocks scraping together, and the shelf she was standing on lurched. It came away from the wall and, devastatingly slowly, began to topple into the Maw. Winter's paws slipped on the ice. She made a desperate leap for the broken shelf. Her front claws found purchase in the ice and she dangled for a moment.

Then the ice that had cracked broke off from the rock entirely, and with a yowl, Winter fell.

The air, already full of the roar of the quaking rocks, was split with the screams of all four cubs Born of Winter as their mother plummeted into the darkness. She twisted in the air, and for a sickly, hopeful second Ghost thought she might be all right, she might land on her feet and be able to climb back up—

But she struck a rock on the way down, and when her body hit the faint line of snow far below, it was with a very final, soft *thump*.

"Mother!" the cubs screamed.

Ghost roared wordlessly, loud enough that the rumbling of the earth almost seemed to soften. He fell to his belly in the snow. Winter was lost, swallowed forever in the Endless Maw.

# CHAPTER SIXTEEN

"AHA!" RAIN POUNCED ON the small bamboo shoot, carefully breaking it off and putting it with the others. It was perfect for Maple. He was still recovering from being all alone—and from his ordeal with the monkeys—and Rain was happy to fetch him his favorite food. She quite liked the little fluff-ball. And she was determined to keep an eye on him too, even though the monkeys hadn't been back and Sunset hadn't shown any more interest in the cub. Whatever he was looking for, it seemed that he'd decided Maple wasn't it.

Which was good, but sort of annoying, too.

*Bargaining with monkeys for special bamboo that doesn't do anything... having them beat up cubs for no reason... what do you want, Sunset Deepwood?*

She carried the small pile of bamboo shoots back to Peony's sleeping place, where she and Dawn were sitting with Maple,

Frog, and Fir. She bumped noses with the cubs before heading back down the hill. She was sniffing for more shoots, but also for any trace of the monkeys. If she could just work out what exactly was in it for Brawnshanks . . .

"Rain."

Rain froze, then turned to smile at Sunset on the ridge above her, feeling embarrassed that she'd just been thinking about catching him, even though she knew he couldn't read her mind.

"Hello, Speaker," she said.

It was hard to look at him, now that she knew just how much he was lying. Part of her wanted to avoid his attention altogether, and part of her wanted to stare and stare at that friendly-elder-panda face with its seemingly sweet and wise nature until she saw where he was hiding his lies.

Sunset strolled down the slope toward her. She forced herself to smile cheerfully.

"How is the search for a crossing coming along?" Sunset asked.

"Not much better yet, I'm afraid," Rain began. "I think there might be a spot near the big gingko tree on the sunrise side of the Prosperhill, but I need to compare the water levels at different times of day and—"

"Rain, can I ask you a question?" Sunset interrupted. Rain's ears pricked up in surprise.

"Of course, Dragon Speaker."

"Why are you lying to me?"

Rain felt as if she'd been pushed into cold water. It seemed for a second as if all the noises of the forest had suddenly been muted. The faint sense of control she'd found by being secretly sarcastic to him vanished like mist at Long Light.

Sunset held her gaze steadily. Rain knew she'd already hesitated too long, that her silence was as good as a confession. The problem was, she couldn't think of an excuse. It wasn't the right time to confront him about *his* lies. And what other reason would she have for ignoring his orders?

"How did you know?" she muttered, trying to buy time while she scrabbled to get a grip.

"Pebble told me you've been nowhere near the river," Sunset said mildly.

Rain's temper flared, jolting her out of her hesitation. "Wow, you've really turned him against me, haven't you?" she snapped. She regretted it instantly. *Not smart, Rain, not smart at all . . .*

But Sunset shook his head as if the accusation had only made him feel slightly sad.

"I'm sorry you feel that," he said, his voice dripping with concern. "I'm interested in why you didn't do as you were asked, though. Did you just not feel like it? Pebble did say that you could be . . . self-motivated."

*Selfish,* Rain thought. *He said* selfish—*and he's wrong. If I were selfish, I wouldn't care whether Sunset was telling the truth or not; I'd go along with it just like the rest.*

"But I promise you," Sunset went on, "all I want is to look after the Bamboo Kingdom. Will you come with me to the river now?" he added. "There's something I'd like to show you. Perhaps it will change your mind."

Part of Rain wondered how he'd react if she just told him no. But on the other hand, what did he want to show her? If he was about to reveal another clue to his strange behavior, without knowing it, then it would be worth the discomfort of walking with him.

". . . All right." Rain said. She didn't think there was much else to say. Sunset turned and, looking over his shoulder, led the way downhill toward the riverbank.

As they walked, she kicked herself—if she'd been as clever as she thought she was, she would actually have gone swimming, so it would have looked like she was doing as he'd asked.

"The thing is, I didn't look for a way across because . . . because there isn't one," she improvised, as they made their way down between the trees. "I've been swimming in this river all my life. I know. The central tide's fatal, no matter how far you go. I just didn't want to tell you the truth; I thought you were going to be disappointed. It seemed so important to you."

"So you were thinking of my feelings," Sunset said. "That was kind of you, but please, don't feel you need to do that anymore. I want you to tell me the truth."

*I bet you do,* Rain thought.

"So . . . why are you so desperate to get to the other side, anyway?" she asked. "Maybe if I'd understood, I'd have tried harder."

"Reuniting with our lost families and friends is the most important thing we can do, isn't it?" Sunset said. "But beyond that, what if the Great Dragon were to send me a vision of some terrible accident about to happen in the Northern Forest, and there were no pandas there for me to pass it on to? The creatures there would be doomed without pandas to pass on the Dragon's warnings."

Rain nodded thoughtfully, but the more she considered this explanation, the less sense it made.

*So which is it? You're so sure we'll find pandas over there, but if that's true, wouldn't they be able to go to their sacred places or whatever and receive your messages, just like they did before the flood?* she thought. *Unless you don't actually have visions at all. Unless you know that you couldn't send a warning to pandas over there anyway.*

Part of her longed to turn and challenge him on all of this. It stung her that Sunset might think she was just as gullible as the rest. But she told herself again that it was much too soon. She would have to play along and buy back his trust somehow.

And anyway, what was he going to show her by the river? She wanted to know, but she felt uneasy, as if all her fur from tail to nose had been ruffled the wrong way and now it couldn't quite lie flat.

They came at last to a point on the riverbank where a flat shelf of rock sloped smoothly down into the shallows. Dappled shadows from the trees overhead reflected on the surface of the water and cast shimmering patterns on the rock beneath. As they approached, a frog let out a croak and hopped from the rock into the river with a soft plop.

Rain's heart lightened a little. This was the place where she had first learned to swim. The gentle slope of the rock was perfect for little paws to get used to the water. She'd met Pebble here a lot too, when they were small cubs. He used to be so afraid of the river he wouldn't even drink from it, but Rain had shown him that he could touch it, and even swim in it, without anything terrible happening. The memory was so warm and full of love . . .

Then she remembered that it was Sunset by her side now, not Pebble, and she shuddered. It felt so wrong for him to be here, though he couldn't have known how important this place was to her.

Sunset padded out into the water and motioned for Rain to come to his side.

All the muscles in Rain's body tensed. She suddenly felt very aware of how large he was. He acted like a friendly elder, but he was a full-grown adult bear, and his travels in the kingdom seemed to have made him strong.

But she didn't have much of a choice. She stepped into the water. The cool river lapped over her paws, coming up to her belly. At any other moment it would have been calming and familiar.

"Look down into the water," Sunset said.

Rain looked at Sunset. He gave her an encouraging nod. She looked down.

The rock under their paws was smooth and black, and the water flowing over it was clear.

"See," Sunset said. His voice dropped a little and he spoke in a deep, wise-sounding tone that reverberated in his chest.

"See the vision that the Great Dragon has given me. Look into the water. You'll see yourself, standing by my side. The Great Dragon has plans for us both, together. It wants you to be my second-in-command, Rain."

Rain looked down. The surface of the water was calm, and she could see her reflection, and Sunset's beside it.

She couldn't help herself. She burst out laughing.

"Just how stupid do you think I am?"

"What?" Sunset's voice returned to its normal pitch as he stared at her in shock.

"Seriously? Did you really think that would work?" Rain splashed her paw through the reflection, and it splintered and reformed exactly the same. "It's showing us together because you're standing right beside me! You really have the others so well trained they'd believe anything, don't you?"

"How dare you," Sunset said coldly, the edge of a growl in his voice. "You should show your Dragon Speaker more respect!"

"I would, if they were here," Rain snapped back. The look on Sunset's face was priceless, but now her laughter was fading and anger filled her heart. How dare he try to trick her like this?

The fury was made all the sharper by the dawning realization that she had done exactly what she had been determined not to do—she had accused him of being a fraud. *Not smart. But I don't care.* There was no turning back now.

"You're a liar and a fraud, Sunset Deepwood. I know you

made a bargain with the monkeys. I know you were the one who had them beat up Maple. And I know you're no Dragon Speaker."

Sunset said nothing. He was shaking with rage, his teeth slowly baring as Rain went on. She took a step away from him, splashing in the shallow water.

"I've waited too long to tell the others what I know, but now I think I should go and lay it out for them. We'll see what they say, shall—"

Sunset leaped.

Panic flared in Rain's chest as she dodged away from him. *He wouldn't—*

Sunset reared up on his back legs and roared. Throwing off all pretense at friendliness, he was suddenly huge in front of Rain, his large adult claws swiping through the air and missing Rain's nose by a hair's breadth.

Why had she thought he wouldn't hurt her?

*Go!*

She tried to turn away. She was smaller, but she was also the better swimmer. If she could just get out into the stream—

Heavy paws came down on her shoulders, and her legs slipped and buckled on the wet stone. She tried to gasp in a deep breath, but she only succeeded in getting a mouthful of water as Sunset forced her under. She tried to brace and roll him off, but her paws scrabbled and she couldn't get a grip on the sandy stone riverbed. Sunset was too strong. Her lungs began to burn as panic blinded her. She tried to fight—she wouldn't be drowned; she of all pandas would *not* let this traitor *drown* her—but as she thrashed, the world dimmed. Sunset's paws were clamped on the sides of her head, keeping her down. She could hear her heartbeat like a slow thunder-clap between her ears, feel it slowing in her throat even as her mind raced, screaming at her body to struggle, to swim, to *do something*.

Then her paw struck an unfamiliar texture. What was it? She couldn't see, couldn't think. It felt like soft flesh, like a fish, but long and wavering like a weed. It wrapped itself around her front paws, and with a feeling like she was falling from a great height, it yanked her forward and down, and out of Sunset's grip.

In her relief, she let go of the last bubble of air she had been holding.

She was free. But she knew she was drowning. And the curling thing around her paws was dragging her deeper and deeper, toward the deadly tide at the center of the flooded river.

# CHAPTER SEVENTEEN

"HYACINTH?" LEAF ROARED. "SEEKER?" Her cry echoed from the sides of the mountain, and she paused, balancing on a pile of rocks, listening for any hint of a reply—a word, a whimper, even the sound of crackling branches. But there was nothing.

"Wanderer? Hunter?" Dasher cried, running out to the end of a tree branch and peering over at the drop down to the bottom of the ravine below. "Is *anybody* out there?"

Leaf held her breath.

A sound caught her ear—a rattling of stones. She and Dasher looked at each other and turned to run toward it, but Leaf already knew it probably wasn't one of their friends. A live panda would have heard them calling and replied. Sure enough, it was just another tumble of loose rocks settling into their new position.

The earth had roared for a long time, but finally it had gone still. The dust had blown away, and now the mountainside looked very different. Most of the thornbushes had been torn up. Broken bamboo and fallen trees were scattered down the slope. And there was no sign of the pandas, or the red pandas.

"If they were dead, we would have found them," Dasher said, for the third time.

He was right, Leaf thought. But it was strangely little comfort. They had been all the way down to the bottom of the hill, where they had seen their friends and family tumble and vanish into the dust clouds. There wasn't, as Leaf had feared, a pile of bodies. But apart from a few scraps of torn fur, there was no sign that the others had even been there—they had disappeared.

"They must have found a way out of danger," she declared, nodding to Dasher. "It seems like they managed to stay together."

"But . . . what do we do now?" Dasher sat down on a wobbly rock, cleaning the dust from behind his ears with his paws. "We have no idea where they've gone, so which way do we go to find them?" He looked to the left and then to the right, following the line of the mountain downward to the next peak.

Leaf stood up and shook herself.

"Up," she said. Dasher turned to stare at her. "If we try to chase after them and go the wrong way, we'll be lost," she said. "The only thing we can do now is carry on—toward the Dragon Mountain. We must try to find Aunt Plum. The others know that's where we were going—if they're still trying to get there too, then we'll find them."

"I suppose you're right," Dasher said in a small voice. Then he brightened. "At least I can't smell that tiger anywhere now."

"Let's eat," said Leaf. "There's all this broken bamboo; we shouldn't waste it. Then we'll go."

Dasher nodded, and scampered off to search the scattered plant life for something tasty for himself while Leaf carefully picked her way across the ground, tearing the leaves and shoots from the fallen bamboo. They climbed back to the top of the ridge before eating, and sat looking out over the Bamboo Kingdom. Leaf couldn't help still listening for rustling or familiar voices, but the whole kingdom seemed to have sunk into a shocked, exhausted silence. When she raised her voice to deliver the blessing, it sounded shaky and thin to her own ears.

"At the Feast of . . ." *Oh no,* she thought, *I'm not even sure what feast this is.* She looked up at the clear sky. Was it Long Light? They had been waiting for the earth to stop roaring for what felt like a long time. Perhaps it was closer to Sun Fall?

"Great Dragon, at the Feast of Sun Fall your humble panda bows before you. Thank you for the gift of the bamboo, and the clarity you bestow upon us."

*I need all the clarity I can get,* she thought.

The feast did give her a little more energy, but the climb up toward the White Spine Mountains was still hard. Leaf felt as though there were a thick vine tethering her to the other pandas, wherever they were, and it tugged on her as she put one shaky paw in front of the other. She tried to shake it off and focus on the route ahead of her.

The air grew colder, but the exertion of the journey kept her warm for a while, until she paused to look back down the way they'd come. All of a sudden, she realized just how far they were from the Slenderwood and the river. The sparse bamboo and tall, leafy trees of her old home looked like a lush, teeming paradise when she compared it to the ridge where she stood now, which was rocky and bare and covered in frost.

They had made it to the base of the White Spine. Sure enough, not long after she had looked back, she began to feel the cold creeping under her fur, no matter how fast she tried to walk to shake it off. Dasher started to shiver, and tucked his thick tail close to his body to shield him from a breeze that carried the first droplets of ice-cold rain.

They walked through a small, dark valley between high crags, and found themselves pushing through and around snowdrifts that had collected there, perhaps thrown down from the higher slopes by the shaking of the earth. Dasher's short legs struggled, and though Leaf was getting tired, she let him ride on her back until they managed to climb up and out of the shadow and onto the rocks.

The rain blew harder and colder, turning into a full, driving sleet that settled in her fur like snow just for a second before melting. There was ice on the ground now as they climbed ever higher, and Leaf decided she preferred the real snowdrifts, however hard they had been to walk on—she tried to watch where she was putting her paws, but the sleet got into her eyes and slicked down her fur. She slipped and fell flat on her belly, letting out a wincing howl.

"Leaf!" Dasher called through the howling wind. "Are you all right?"

"Fine," Leaf grumbled. A rock had jabbed her in the ribs, and every part of her was soaked through and ice cold. She got back to her paws and shuddered, then looked around. They were standing on a field of broken rock and ice, which sloped gently upward to meet a cliff that looked like a wall of enormous boulders piled one on top of another.

"We could climb that," Leaf told Dasher, pointing out the cliff. "Take the shortcut. But not in this weather . . ."

"We've got to find somewhere to get out of the wind." Dasher crept in close to her side.

*Are you using me as a shelter?* Leaf thought, but she didn't chide him aloud—frankly, she couldn't blame him. Anything between her and the swirling, worsening weather would have been welcome.

"We'll have to keep going along here. Maybe there'll be a cave in the cliff," Leaf told him. Dasher groaned, and she bent down and licked the drenched fur on his face so that it at least wasn't falling in his eyes so much.

She knew it wouldn't do much good, even though he stuck to her side as they walked. It wasn't long before both of them were drenched and moving clumsily over the rocks as their legs grew stiff from cold. Leaf felt like she was actually wetter than she had been after they'd both fallen in the river.

They were also running out of hillside, the rocky field growing thinner and the steep cliff face coming closer. Leaf was just starting to think that they might have to attempt to climb the slick, sharp rocks in the wind and sleet after all, when she saw something up ahead. A circle of tall rocks sticking up from the ground, like the claws of a paw, or an open roaring mouth full of teeth. They made a stark and slightly scary sight against the cloudy sky, but also formed a sort of half cave, with one wide rock claw leaning over so that the inside would be at least slightly sheltered from the sky.

"It's perfect," Dasher yelped, and broke into a run.

"Careful!" Leaf called after him, just as his paws slithered on a patch of ice. He tumbled over, but got up again at once.

"I'm okay! Come on, let's get inside!" Dasher hurried, a little more carefully, toward the tall rocks.

The closer they got, the more Leaf could see how big the formation really was. It would be wonderful to be out of the wind, sheltered from this bleak and barren landscape. But there was something she didn't like about this spot, a chill that didn't have anything to do with the frozen ground under her paws.

Dasher paused as he reached the gap between the stones. He looked over his shoulder and blinked through the sleet at Leaf as she joined him.

"It is a bit . . . eerie, right?" he said.

"Yeah." Leaf put her nose through the gap and sniffed. It smelled as strange as everything did up here on the mountain: of ice and rock and the odd, faint trail of passing creatures. She stepped over the threshold into the sheltered space, trying to ignore the feeling that she was stepping into the mouth of a giant beast. Dasher followed her in.

The sheltered area inside was large enough for both of them to stand and turn without bumping into each other, and it really was a relief to be out of the wind, though the sleet fell in wet drips through the gaps in the stone.

Dasher sat down and began to paw at his face and ears, wiping away some of the wetness, but Leaf couldn't get comfortable. She paced around the edge, sniffing at the rocks.

"There's something . . ." She couldn't finish the thought—she didn't know what it was she was sensing.

She looked down at Dasher. He was still pawing at his ears, though they were already clean. He shuddered.

"I can feel it too," he said. "Do you think we'd be better off out there?"

"Maybe . . ." Leaf turned to look out through the gap in the stones.

But something was in the gap, blocking the way out. For a moment, she couldn't see it clearly in the dying light.

Then she let out a howl of fear and leaped backward, stumbling over her own paws and falling onto her haunches. Dasher skittered around to look, yelped, and crouched low to the ground as the tiger stepped slowly in through the gap in the stones.

Close up he was huge, bigger than the biggest of the pandas. His head was held high, his bright yellow eyes fixed on Leaf. His muzzle twitched as he sniffed at her, and she flinched and clumsily scrambled up and backed away until she struck the stone wall hard with a back paw.

*The wind. The sleet. I didn't scent him coming.*

She certainly scented him now. The predator's reek of torn flesh filled her nostrils and sent her heart rattling in her chest as the big cat put another paw forward, and then another. His striped fur rippled across his shoulders, sleek but powerful.

He was blocking the only way out.

*This will be over quickly.*

Down by her paws, Dasher pressed into the stone, his fur fluffed up and a high-pitched, panicky growl coming from between his bared teeth. Leaf wanted to stand her ground with him, until the end, to make herself look fearsome. She was a bear! She had big teeth and big claws and—

And she had never been in a fight, not ever. She hadn't even liked to play-fight as a little cub.

*We're going to die.*

The tiger sniffed again, and Leaf jumped and whimpered.

She was no fighter. But perhaps she could buy Dasher time. Maybe he could make it through one of the gaps in the stones high above.

*O Great Dragon, why? Why have you brought us here? Why . . . why hasn't it attacked yet?*

The tiger was just . . . *watching* them. At last his mouth opened, revealing a glimpse of sharp fangs. But instead of sinking them into Leaf's neck, the tiger spoke, in a voice that resonated deep within his chest and seemed to fill the hollow place between the stones.

"You," he said. His gaze was still trained on Leaf, the black pupils wide in the dim light. "You are the panda with one white pad."

Leaf couldn't answer for several moments. How could you hold a conversation with a creature that might be about to eat you? But at last the tiger's words settled in her mind. Almost involuntarily, she lifted her paw and looked down at it. There were her pads, all black apart from the larger grip pad, which was white.

The tiger's ears twitched as he saw it too. Leaf flinched, bracing herself for the leap and bite . . . but instead the tiger sat back on his haunches.

"I have been searching for you for a long time," he said.

"Why?" Dasher yelped. He was still fluffed up and pressed tight against Leaf's flank. "What do you want Leaf for?"

"I have come to honor a promise I made to another panda, during the great flood. You needn't tremble, small fox-bear," he added. "I won't eat you if this panda—Leaf—asks me not to."

"Please," Leaf squeaked. She tried to clear her throat. "Dasher's my friend. I can't trust you unless you promise not to hurt either of us."

"A tiger's promise is not easily given, but it is always kept," said the creature. He paused for a moment, and then raised a paw to clean his whiskers, in a movement that oddly reminded Leaf of Dasher. "Leaf the panda. Dasher the fox-bear. My name is Shadowhunter. And I promise I will not hurt either one of you."

Leaf still felt deeply uncertain about this, despite the tiger's assurances, and she was sure Dasher would be thinking of poor Scratcher. But she didn't have much of a choice.

She forced herself to sit down. Outside, the wind still howled and the sleet pattered against the standing stones.

"Well, you've found me. What promise did you make during the flood?"

"I promised to find you, when the time was right, and tell you who you are. This I promised your mother."

Leaf had been about to shoot back that she knew who she was, thank you, but now she froze, mouth open.

"Orchid Risingtree chose my cave to shelter in during the storm, as the flood swirled below. She delivered her cubs in my den. I was there when you were born—you and your two littermates."

*My what?*

*What do you mean, two littermates?*

*We've met before?*

*What do you mean, "who I am"?*

Leaf tried to speak, but she had so many questions they all seemed to cram together in her throat, keeping her silent. She could only stare at Shadowhunter. None of this made any sense. This couldn't be happening.

And yet the tiger's terrifying appearance seemed to shift and change with every word. He had known her mother. He had known *her*, as a tiny, helpless cub. He didn't actually shrink, but every moment he didn't attack them, he seemed less like a monster.

"No, Leaf just has one littermate," Dasher whispered. "We know that . . . don't we? That's what Plum always said. What happened to the other one, if there were three? Did

you do something to them? Like you *ate* my uncle Scratcher?"
he added, growling at Shadowhunter. Shadowhunter growled
in return, his lips peeling back to show his long, sharp fangs.
Each one was about the length of Dasher's entire skull.

"I would never hurt the triplets," he snarled. "I gave Orchid
my word I would protect them all, whatever the cost."

"Then where are they?" Leaf found her voice at last. "My
other two littermates? And my mother, where is she?"

Shadowhunter stopped growling. He sat and licked his jaws
with a pink tongue as wide as two of Leaf's paws side by side.

"You are the first I've found. You had to be separated after
you were born, for your own safety. You had to be hidden,
and have your destiny hidden, even from you. If other creatures understood what you were, some of them would try to
use you—or kill you. But now is the time." Shadowhunter's
eyes gleamed in the darkness, and for a moment he stared into
the air above her head, as if he could see something there she
could not. "The Great Dragon walks among us," he said, his
voice rumbling low in his chest. "Its breath is at our backs."

Leaf shivered. She thought of the sensation she'd felt on
the hillside—the sinuous black shape in the undergrowth, and
the warm breeze in her fur. . . .

"Destiny is on the move, and it has chosen you: all three of
you. The triplets born of Orchid are the new Dragon Speakers."

# CHAPTER EIGHTEEN

GHOST LAY WHERE HE had fallen, a few staggering steps away from the edge of the Endless Maw. Snow fell steadily, and he didn't move to shake it off. He let it cover his nose and the ends of his paws.

Winter was dead.

The only mother he'd known, or ever would.

*Did I tell her I loved her? All I wanted was to stay here, with her. Did she know?*

He couldn't remember. He searched his mind, but there was a yawning darkness where their last conversation should have been. He knew he'd yelled at her. He'd been harsh, he was sure of it, even though she was trying to explain that she'd done her best. But he couldn't remember the words.

The sound of the ledge cracking, the sight of Winter falling, those were sharp and clear in his memory—he couldn't *stop* remembering them. They were like bolts of lightning crackling across the sky, striking again and again. It made no difference whether his eyes were open or closed; he could still see her falling.

"Mother," Shiver kept repeating. She was lying in the snow with her chin resting on the edge of the Maw, staring down and mewling under her breath, as if she couldn't stop herself. "Mother, please come back. Mother, please."

Snowstorm and Frost were a little way away, huddled together. Their grief was quiet, like the mountain after the shaking of the earth had stopped. They muttered a few words to each other in low, haunted voices.

*You belong with me,* she'd said.

It was true. Ghost belonged with Winter—at the bottom of the crevasse.

*She gave her life to save me, but she should have left me there. They all should have.*

"Shiver," he heard Snowstorm say. "Stop."

Ghost turned his head and saw Snowstorm seize her small sister by the scruff of the neck and bodily lift her away from the edge of the crevasse.

"She's gone. You have to stop." Snowstorm deposited Shiver in the snow, and then turned to look at Ghost.

Neither the snow nor the ice nor the darkness of the Endless Maw was as cold as the look in Snowstorm's eyes as she and Frost trod across the snow to stand side by side, looking down at Ghost. Frost's ears were pinned back in misery, and his breath was coming in shuddering gasps. Next to him,

Snowstorm was completely still, as if she'd been carved from the rock of the mountain. When she finally spoke, her voice was low and hoarse.

"This is your fault," she said. "Mother is dead. And it's your fault. If she hadn't had to save you from your own stupid tantrum, she would still be here."

Her words cut into him, like falling shards of rock. Ghost sat up.

"I know," he whispered.

For a moment, silent misery swirled around all three of them like the falling snow.

"You're—it was so *stupid*," Frost quavered. "You're always trying to do things you know you can't. You *knew* you couldn't jump the Maw. You should have died. I don't know what you thought would happen."

"Mother loved you so much," Snowstorm added, her voice still low and freakishly calm. "She always loved you the best. She always spent all her time worrying about you, never about any of us. She should have been taking care of Shiver, but you were always more important. You're so useless at everything, but you would never just stop trying to keep up. She thought you were so special. But you're not. You're just not one of us. You're just . . . a *bear*. And you killed our mother."

Ghost shut his eyes and let her words pummel against him. She was right. It was all his fault. He—

"Are you listening to me, *freak?*" Snowstorm yowled. Her voice broke, and Ghost opened his eyes in time to see her rearing back, fangs bared and claws out, ready to swipe across his face. "You killed my mother!"

Her muscles bunched, ready to spring. Ghost didn't move. He waited for the impact, but it didn't come. A smaller blur of spotted fur barreled into Snowstorm, throwing her off balance. Shiver head-butted her sister under the chin, not very hard, but with a fierceness that startled Ghost.

"Don't hurt him!" Shiver yelled. "He's our brother! It's not his fault the ground roared! It's not his fault he's a bear!"

"It is!" Snowstorm mewled, and Ghost's fur prickled with dismay as her aggressive posture dropped and she sat back, shaking her head over and over again and kneading the ground in front of her. "It has to be, or—or what—what are we going to do now?"

She dropped to her belly in the snow, turned her face to the sky, and let out a yowl of grief. Frost backed away, looking as if he might lose control too at any moment.

Ghost couldn't bear it. It had been better when they'd wanted to hurt him.

"You're right," he said. He got up and shook the snow from his fur. "Snowstorm, listen. You're right. It's my fault. I'm a freak, a—a bear. Just like those sun bears said."

Shiver and Frost stared at Ghost, confusion mingling with their grief.

"How?" Frost whimpered.

"You're still our brother," said Shiver, in a low and shaky voice.

"I'm not," Ghost almost snapped at Shiver. She had to understand the truth. "Mother told me what really happened.

She found me in a cave. I don't know where I came from, but I'm not supposed to be here. I don't belong in the mountains. So I'll . . ."

He took a deep breath, looking at Snowstorm. She had calmed a little, but it seemed like she still couldn't speak. She looked up at Ghost with huge, liquid eyes.

"I'll go," he said. "I'll go away, forever, and you'll never have to see me again."

He didn't let himself hesitate a moment longer. He wouldn't wait for them to agree—or to ask him to stay. If he was going to be alone, he would choose it for himself.

He turned, and took his first steps away from his family.

"No, Ghost . . . ," Shiver mewed, but Ghost ignored her. He walked away, stumbling over his first few steps, but forcing himself to keep going. He wouldn't look back. He wouldn't take a last look at the cubs Born of Winter, or the Maw that had swallowed her.

He focused on what was in front of him—a long, snow-covered hill, the distant shadows of trees. He fixed his eyes on a rock, then on a tree, thinking, *I can make it that far. My paws can take me that much farther.*

He descended a series of rocky steps, away from the snow-field and into the shade of a patch of trees. He only stopped walking when he knew for certain that if he turned around he wouldn't see the leopards behind him. He looked back, and only saw the rocks he'd climbed down.

Then he sank down to his haunches, leaning against one of the tree trunks, and squeezed his eyes shut. He wanted to howl and roar, but he wouldn't let the others know how he was feeling.

*Snow Cat . . .*, he thought, then stopped.

Why would the Snow Cat care about him, if he wasn't even a cat?

But the Snow Cat *had* helped him. It had shown him the way to the deer. That had *happened*, and he was just as sure of it now as he had ever been.

"Why did you do that?" he groaned aloud. "I don't understand. Why would you help me then, but let Winter die? Snow Cat . . . I don't know what to do. I've never left the mountains. I don't know where I'm going, or what I'll do when I get there. . . ." He had to stop, his voice choking on his despair. Finally he sniffed and went on. "Snow Cat, please leave your footprints for me now. I need them more than ever."

There was no warm breath in response, no change in the dim light.

Ghost had to carry on alone.

He had never been on a journey like this before. He wasn't hunting, or going on a walk with his littermates that would end, eventually, back at their cave. There was no destination in his mind. The only direction, always, was *down*. If a slope was shallow enough for him to walk down it, he did so. It was easier than climbing, but after a while the constant descent started to make his knees wobble, and he had to stop and rest at the edge of a cliff.

The day was drawing to a close. He looked out over the rolling peaks of the mountains, trying to see what was below, but he couldn't make out anything beyond the next hill. Sheets of rain battered the slopes just below him, icy sleet making the rocks slippery. He would need to find somewhere to shelter for the night, and what was worse, his stomach was already rumbling. The cubs hadn't eaten in a day, and Ghost had always felt hunger more keenly than the others.

*Perhaps bears aren't supposed to eat like leopards. We clearly can't hunt the same way as leopards. . . . But then how do we do it?*

He had no idea. He knew he didn't know how to be a leopard, but how could he ever learn to be a bear instead? He sighed, and got up to push on. It was all he could do. Perhaps he would find a dying creature, or the remains of someone else's kill. Even some nuts or berries would keep him alive a little longer, if he could find any in the bare, rocky land around the lower slopes of the White Spine.

He started walking along the cliff edge, searching for the best way down. Then he stopped. He heard something moving. Something behind him . . .

"Ghost!"

Ghost spun around and stared as a white, spotted shape came bounding between the trees.

It was Shiver.

"I found you!" she mewed. "There you are!" She trotted to a halt and sat down, her breath coming in gasps and her tail twitching happily.

The sight of her warmed Ghost's heart. He had only been gone a little while, but he had thought he would never see her again. Her familiar face made him feel, just for a moment, as if he were home again. As if everything was going to be all right.

"What are you doing here?" he asked. "You should be back with the others."

"No." Shiver shook her head. "I'm coming with you. You're my brother, no matter where you came from or—or what's happened."

Ghost swallowed. "Shiver . . . what about Snowstorm and Frost? What about the mountain?"

"They weren't happy," Shiver said, dipping her head. Her expression twisted with regret for a moment; then her frown turned determined, and she looked up at Ghost again. "But I know it's the right thing to do. I . . . I won't ever jump the Maw either," she said. Ghost opened his mouth to protest, but she glared at him. "You know it's true. I'm just too small and too weak. Perhaps neither of us really belongs here, no matter who our parents were. But we're littermates, and I'm not going to let you go alone."

Ghost let out a heavy sigh and trotted forward to lean his head against Shiver's. She pressed back, closing her eyes.

"Mother wouldn't want you to be alone," Shiver whispered.

Ghost's breath came shakily as they stood there together, remembering Winter.

Then he pulled away and gave Shiver a hard, affectionate lick on the top of her head.

"Then let's go," he said. "Together."

Shiver purred and butted her head against his shoulder, and they set off, side by side.

They found a shallow streambed that cut through the cliff and made their way down, their paws splashing and slipping on the wet stones. Shiver pointed out another clump of trees just down the hill, and they headed for them. Ghost hoped that they might provide some cover, perhaps even for the night—the warmth in his heart from having his sister by his side wasn't going away, but it also wasn't doing much to stop the cold wind from chilling the end of his nose.

Unfortunately, they got to the trees at the same time as a sweeping blast of freezing sleet. The trunks were too far apart, and all they did was shower Ghost and Shiver in frozen pine needles as well as slushy ice. They kept walking, preferring to press head-on into the weather than try to get a miserable night's sleep somewhere with no shelter.

Night drew in, and the sleet didn't seem to be letting up any time soon, but the two littermates didn't know what else to do but keep going. Ghost noticed that the lower slopes of the White Spine were showing more and more signs of the terrible shaking that had thrown Winter to her doom: cracks in the ground tripped him, trees lay across the path, and bushes that might have made a cold but workable shelter had been torn from their roots and scattered across the slope.

They walked on through the dark, sniffing and feeling their way along the rocks. The sleet still fell, and heavy clouds covered the moon.

Then, suddenly, Ghost felt Shiver stop walking. He looked around and could just make out the twitch of movement as her ears pricked up.

"What is it?" he asked.

"I think I see something." She turned and trotted away, and Ghost hurried after her, keen not to lose the faint shape of her tail swishing in front of him. "Yes! Look, it's a cave!"

Ghost squinted, and then out of the darkness loomed a cliff face, and, sure enough, there was definitely a dark, open space. He let out a heavy huff of relief. They might go hungry tonight, but thanks to Shiver, at least they would be able to rest out of the wind and the sleet. He shook himself, and they stepped together into the mouth of the cave.

It was blessedly dry, even a few paw steps inside, and it seemed deep. Farther in, it would be even warmer! Ghost padded forward, his heart so full of gladness to be out of the weather that it was only after he was all the way inside that he thought to sniff the air.

There was a scent there, the scent of another creature. The cave was already occupied.

He tensed. Then he heard a skittering of claws on stone, and something growled.

Ghost threw himself in front of Shiver as the thing barged toward him in the darkness. It was bigger than him, and it was *strange*—it seemed almost like a bundle of unconnected parts. A white paw, half a white face, white front and back legs, snapping teeth: It moved as one creature, but it looked terrifyingly disjointed. He roared with fear and swiped out hard in front of him. His claws caught, and raked through fur and flesh.

The creature let out a terrible, wounded cry. It skittered around Ghost and Shiver, and Ghost spun to follow it, in case it tried to get to his littermate. But it just ran past them and out into the cold night. Ghost followed it to the mouth of the cave, growling. This was his cave now! This monstrous thing should run far, far away!

But as it emerged from the total darkness into the faintly moonlit night, he realized what he'd been seeing—not a collection of white parts, but a whole creature that was white with black markings on its face and across its back.

It was a bear. Just like him, but larger and heavier, with patches of black fur where all Ghost had was white.

It staggered away and vanished into the gloom, whining in pain.

"Thank you, Ghost!" Shiver mewed, pressing her trembling body against his shoulder. "That thing was so strange! It might have eaten me!"

He licked the top of her head. She was right; he had done the right thing. He'd protected his family.

But as Ghost sat back on his haunches, he looked down at his paw and saw his claws dripping with the other bear's blood, dark red smeared across the stone—the same color that must surely have seeped from Winter's body, staining the snow at the bottom of the Maw. . . .

A slow horror crept into his heart.

*Will I always have blood on my paws?*

# CHAPTER NINETEEN

RAIN DRIFTED THROUGH GREEN fog. Stones and fish and weeds swirled around her, passing in flashes of gold and silver and blue and white. She thought she was sinking, deeper and deeper into the river, into the very heart of the Bamboo Kingdom. Her pulse was a slow, persistent thump in her ears.

The thing that had coiled around her paw was still there. She could feel its hold on her, firm and solid no matter how slick her fur got or how fast it pulled her through the current.

She knew she would drown. But her heart gave a hard, painful lurch as she thought of Sunset's attack, his lies. She felt one final burst of fury at the injustice of it all. . . .

Then she was being tugged upward, and her head broke the surface. She gulped in a lungful of air, water splashing up her nose and into her eyes. Above the water was a blur of white clouds and green branches, splintered wood floating along beside her. But as soon as she had caught her breath and spat out a mouthful of water, she felt the coiled thing tighten around her paw, pulling her back down again. This time she was almost ready for it, and she snorted and closed her eyes as the river closed back over her head.

She couldn't fight against the thing that dragged her along—she couldn't even see it. She flew through the water now, faster and faster, and it seemed as if she were flying through the sky, over a landscape of deep valleys and waving trees. She could see clearly, all the way to the very bottom of the river.

There was something down there that wasn't stone, and wasn't wood. A lot of white somethings, like a white line cutting right through the kingdom. They filled the channel that must have been the bottom of the original river, before the flood swelled it to its new, monstrous size.

They were bones. She could see skulls, big and small, teeth and claws, long leg bones and tiny finger bones and spines and ribs.

*They are the drowned,* she thought, against the pounding rhythm of her heartbeat. *They are here, all of them. Pandas and monkeys and birds and rats and lizards, all mixed together.*

*The Bamboo Kingdom, united in death . . .*

Her vision finally began to blur. The bones seemed to run together like a liquid stream of pale white. The edges of her sight turned dark, and then black. The world narrowed to a smaller and smaller circle of light.

Something passed across the circle, a shadow of a creature,

walking. Rain's world shifted and changed. She wasn't in the water now. She was standing inside a dark cave, although she couldn't feel the stones under her feet. She felt dry and warm, despite the rain she could hear striking the ground outside.

A movement made her look to her left. A panda stood there, a female. Her teeth were bared in a frightened snarl. She didn't seem to see Rain, only the creature at the mouth of the cave.

It stepped inside, and Rain saw that it was a huge cat, even bigger than a leopard, with fur the color of fire, striped with black.

It was staring at the panda, growling deep in its chest. And then, just for a moment, its eyes shifted, and it fixed its bright yellow gaze on Rain.

She felt something tug at her paw—the coiled force, still there, even though she was no longer in the river—and she seemed to drop through the floor of the cave, right through the stone, and into another world again. She was on a high mountaintop, up to her belly in snow, following a long and winding ridge toward a peak wreathed in clouds. She looked down the mountain and saw the Bamboo Kingdom in impossibly clear detail, all the hills and all the trees, the river sparkling through the middle, bamboo forests thriving on the slopes.

There were two other pandas there, walking the mountain with her. She could see them, but when she tried to looked more closely, she couldn't make out their faces.

She looked back at the peak in front of her. She knew it,

though she had never seen it before: the Dragon Mountain.

The clouds of the dragon's breath swirled faster and faster around the peak, and then suddenly they broke away from the rocks and crashed down the mountain toward her like an avalanche or a tidal wave. The mist hit her, and for a moment she felt nothing but warmth. Then there was an impact that rattled her whole body, and Rain opened her eyes.

She was floating on the surface of the fast-moving river. Another wave slammed into her and she was tossed onto her back.

She was awake now, properly awake. The coiled thing around her paw was gone, and she was alone, caught in the fatal currents of the impassable river. She gulped in several deep breaths and struck out with her paws, trying desperately to right herself in the water. She did it just in time to see a jagged rock cutting through the water right ahead, and managed to throw out her paws and push herself off so it didn't slam into her head or her ribs. Spinning and splashing, she kept her head just above water while more rocks and waves and pieces of debris swirled her around and tried to smack into her.

*Rapids!*

Rain knew there was no way to swim against rapids, not when the river was splitting all the time into a hundred different faster, harder currents. She just had to hold on, and dodge rocks, and not get dragged under again. . . .

*Come on, Rain,* she thought. *You weren't killed by the traitor; you will not be killed by your own river! You're alive, now. Stay alive!*

She spotted something large and brown floating through

the water nearby. A tree trunk, with three huge and twisted branches sticking up out of the water like the heads of snakes.

*Like the thing you saw in the pool . . .*

She shook off that thought. That thought could wait until she had successfully not drowned. She pushed off a rock just as the tree trunk bounced from another, and managed to sink her claws into the wet bark. She pulled herself up, grunting and yelling with the effort, until she could drape herself over the wood, her shoulders at least up out of the water. Rocks and branches of trees whipped past, and some of them struck the trunk and spun it around and around in the water, but Rain held on, growling, *daring* the river to try to drown her one more time. At last she felt herself fall as the tree trunk ran over a rock and dropped down to a lower part of the river, and then, almost at once, the river was calmer, the current slower.

Rain clung on to the trunk a moment longer, catching her breath and waiting for her moment. Finally she rounded a bend in the river and saw a slope of pebbles extending farther into the water than the rest of the land around it.

She took a deep breath and pushed off from the trunk, swimming as hard as she could, though her muscles all screamed at her and she was so tired she could barely breathe. Her claws finally struck rocks, and then pebbles, and finally dug into the soft earth of the beach. She tried to stand, but her limbs were too weak, so she dragged herself on her belly up and away from the water. She coughed, and a stream of water came up, and she spat it out onto the ground.

Then she flopped onto her side, the river still lapping at the tips of her back paws. She glanced back toward the tree trunk she had held on to, expecting to see it floating away down the river.

But instead she saw something dark, that ended in three twisting branches, turn into mist and melt away into the air.

*Still dreaming,* she thought. *Maybe I drowned after all.*

But a part of her knew that wasn't right.

What if it hadn't been her imagination, that day by the pool?

What if she had seen the Great Dragon?

What if that thing that had seized her paw and pulled her away from Sunset was . . .

Rain couldn't hold her head up anymore. She let it fall back onto the beach with a crunch. She couldn't think about any of it—it was too big, and she was too tired. She knew she had to get up, had to pull herself away from the river or it could drag her back in. She didn't know where she was, or what might find her if she didn't move.

She squeezed her eyes shut, trying to find the energy to get up, but she couldn't even open them again. Darkness flowed over her, and she felt warm, and then she felt nothing.

# CHAPTER TWENTY

LEAF SAT BACK ON her haunches, letting the morning sun warm her fur, though up here on the mountain even the brightest sunshine was forced to fight against the chill in the air. Her ears were warming up, at least, and the black stripe of fur across her back.

She held the small tuft of Plum's fur carefully between her paws. With Shadowhunter's help, they had managed to find their way back to the place where they had been separated from the other pandas and red pandas, and Leaf had found the fur still hanging from one of the thorny bushes.

She couldn't believe that she was traveling with a predator, let alone a *tiger*. He was no less frightening in the daylight, although having fallen asleep right beside him and woken up unharmed had been reassuring.

It hadn't reassured Dasher quite so much. He'd slept

pressed between Leaf and the stone wall, and she'd been happy to let him. It wasn't her uncle the tiger had devoured, after all.

A little way away underneath a tree, Shadowhunter yawned, his mouth splitting wide enough to fit Leaf's whole head inside, his enormous tongue lashing out and curling between his massive teeth. Then he reached up to rake his claws down the tree's trunk.

Leaf tried to ignore him, and instead sniffed at the scrap of Plum's fur. The scent was almost gone now, after the rain overnight and the dust from the shaking earth, but Leaf could still make out the warm, familiar smell of her aunt. It made her heart ache.

"She was here," she said. "And if she didn't go the way we went yesterday . . . perhaps she went down the other side here and up the next hill instead?"

Dasher sighed. "The tiger did say he hadn't scented any panda on that slope but you."

Leaf gave him a sympathetic look. His ears had been pinned back, as if they were stuck to the sides of his skull, ever since he'd woken up and found Shadowhunter's gently snoring form still blocking the exit from the cave.

"Come on," she said. "It's time for the Feast of Golden Light. Let's find something to eat."

There was still some bamboo strewn across the slope—it wouldn't be particularly tasty, but it would have to do. There hadn't been anything at all to eat at the Feast of Moon Fall. Leaf had had to stare up at the cloudy sky and ask the Great

Dragon for its blessing, even though she had no bamboo to be thankful for.

Dasher managed to find a fallen trunk full of small insects, and set to work picking them out and crunching on them while Leaf thanked the Great Dragon for her strength. She suspected she would need it today. Afterward, Dasher seemed a little happier, though he still stayed several steps behind her as she stood and approached Shadowhunter. The tiger had curled up and was washing between his paw pads.

"Look at those claws," Dasher muttered. "What happens to us when he decides he's hungry? He won't be satisfied with leaves and insects, will he? We should stay close to the trees, so we can climb out of his reach if he decides to come after us after all."

*I think he can probably climb any tree we can get to,* Leaf thought, but she knew it would do neither of them any good if she said it out loud.

"I really don't think he will break his promise," she murmured instead. "He wouldn't have gone to so much trouble to find us, and tell me everything he told me, just to eat us now."

Dasher made an unconvinced *hmmm* noise.

Shadowhunter saw them coming and got to his feet, stretching out his long, striped back and lashing his strong tail.

"Are you ready, Dragon Speaker?" he asked.

Leaf hesitated.

*Ready to be called that? Absolutely not.*

She had never met a Dragon Speaker, but the Slenderwood pandas had told stories of the great wisdom and kindness of

Sunset Deepwood and his predecessors. They had saved the Bamboo Kingdom over and over again, ever since the pandas and the Great Dragon had come into being. They cared equally for all creatures. They always had an answer to any problem, and if they didn't, they would not rest until they found one.

How could Leaf be one of them? And how could her siblings be Dragon Speakers too? She'd never heard of there being more than one at a time. For that matter, she had never heard of pandas giving birth to triplets, either. Could the tiger be mistaken after all? What if he was lying to her, or had just gotten mixed up?

"I need to find Aunt Plum," she said at last. She held the tuft of fur out to the tiger. "I think you're probably better at tracking than I am. Can you use this scent to find her?"

Shadowhunter sniffed at the fur, almost lifting it from Leaf's palm.

"I shall do my best," he rumbled, standing up. He walked to the bush where it had been hanging, and sniffed there, too. Then he looked over his shoulder. "The trail is faint. We should hurry."

Leaf's heart leaped. They were going to find Aunt Plum, at last! Then she hurried after the tiger, who had taken off at a fast trot and was almost at the crest of the hill already.

Dasher scampered beside her as they followed the swishing tail of the tiger, up and over the hill, down into the little valley on the other side and up the next slope, circling a broken column of rock that stuck up from the side of a hill like a single claw pointing toward the sky. As soon as Leaf made it to the top of that next ridge, she could see that this was a better way to get to the Dragon Mountain—that nearly unclimbable rock wall they'd come up against last night would be below them if they went this way.

There was little shelter, the higher they went, and now the snow on the ground was only broken up by the edges of sharp rocks or small scraps of leafless vegetation. Leaf kept her eyes peeled for tracks, but the snow must have been freshly fallen, because she didn't see any apart from the large cat prints of Shadowhunter.

"I think you'd make a good Dragon Speaker," Dasher said suddenly, as they climbed up a rough slope of snow and loose shale. "I don't know if the tiger's telling us the truth, but I reckon you'd be good at it."

Leaf shook her head. "I don't know. I'm just—I'm so ordinary! I like bamboo and climbing trees and hanging out with you. I'm not a *leader*. Plum would make a much better Dragon Speaker than I would; she's the one who made the decision to go to the Dragon Mountain and find out what was happening."

"Yeah, but you're the one that the Dragon showed the way, when it was dark and we were lost," Dasher said. "No red panda ever got a vision like that, and you can't argue with visions! Anyway, if you want leadership, look at us right now: You've got me following a tiger up a mountain. Aren't many pandas I'd do that for."

"I . . . Dasher, I . . ." Leaf's eyes widened and her heart

swelled, but she couldn't seem to find the words to respond. Instead she bent down and licked the top of Dasher's head.

"Come on," Dasher said, and head-butted her affectionately in the leg. "Or we'll lose him, and a tiger you can see is definitely better than a tiger you can't."

They hurried after Shadowhunter, their paws crunching in the snow.

It was Sun Climb now, but Leaf decided not to stop their journey for a feast. She wasn't sure if that was good Dragon Speaker leadership or more proof that Shadowhunter was mistaken, but she said the blessing privately in her head, thanking the Dragon for the gift of honesty.

*It would be dishonest not to admit that finding Plum is more important than feasting right now,* she thought. She hoped the Dragon understood that.

"Leaf," growled Shadowhunter suddenly. "Something's here."

Leaf put on a burst of speed and ran up the snowy slope to a patch of ferns where the tiger was sniffing intently at the ground. There was a cliff a little farther up and to the right, with a few dark splits in the rock that could have been openings to caves. Was Plum in one of them?

She reached the tiger's side. "What have you found?" she asked him. "Is it a new trail?"

"Blood," said Shadowhunter.

Leaf's heart dropped into her paws as she looked down and saw a spatter of red drops on the white snow.

"Is it . . . does it smell like . . ."

"She was here." Shadowhunter began to pace back and forth quickly, crossing bear-lengths in a few strides, up and down the slope. He stopped and sniffed, came back and sniffed again. Leaf watched him, her heart in her mouth. She wanted to run to the caves. Plum could be in one of them, injured, dying. . . . But she forced herself to trust her strange new ally.

The wait was short but agonizing, until Shadowhunter returned to the spot where she stood frozen.

"She came from the caves, bleeding," he said. "She went that way." He pointed with his nose, through the ferns, toward a clump of leafless trees that jutted out from the side of the hill.

Leaf turned toward them and ran, pushing through the ferns, her eyes on the ground so she wouldn't fall. She saw more spatters of blood pass under her paws as the trees grew closer. Dasher overtook her, his little legs a blur as he scampered ahead.

"Plum!" Leaf roared. The mountain echoed with it. "Plum, are you there?"

Dasher vanished around the side of a big rock, and into the space between the trees, and then—

"Leaf, come quick—she's here!"

Leaf put on a burst of speed. She pushed through another clump of ferns and around the rock and saw what she had been dreading: Aunt Plum, lying still on the ground, blood matting the fur across her face. Leaf's legs felt like snow crumbling in the sun, and she fell forward with a moan of grief.

Then Plum groaned, and looked toward her.

"Leaf . . . ? Is it you . . . ?"

"Plum!" Leaf sprang to her paws and ran to her aunt's side. "You're alive!"

"Yes . . . ," Plum said, but her voice was faint. "I'm alive, I'm alive, yes . . . and Leaf is here, at the end. . . . That's good. . . ."

"It's not the end! I'm here. I can help you," Leaf said. She began to lick the wound on Plum's face, but as she tasted the blood, she shuddered. It smelled bad, like a dead thing that had been left in the sun.

"I was following," said Plum quietly. "Following my heart, following the Dragon . . . I followed to the cave; I followed and waited. There was going to be a sign. But then, in the dark . . . the monster. The white monster. Muscles and teeth, white, like death, like a bear . . . It saw with the eyes of death. . . ."

"Her wound is addling her mind," said Shadowhunter's voice, from behind Leaf. He had climbed up onto the big rock and was lying there, looking down on them with genuine sadness in his eyes. Plum tried to turn her head in the direction of the voice, but she couldn't seem to make him out. "She may last another day, but soon she will be gone. You should say goodbye, while she still knows you."

"No," Leaf moaned.

But at the same time, Dasher said, "No," with stern determination in his small voice. He padded up to Plum's face and sniffed at her wound.

"Dash?" Leaf said, swallowing hard. "Please, is there anything you can do?"

"I—I'm a Climbing Far; I'm no Healing Heart," he said. "But I've seen Forager give red pandas purple leaf, when they get like this. It's a kind of bamboo. . . ." He groaned, and shook his head. Leaf's heart, which had been climbing into her throat, crashed back to the pit of her stomach. "But it only grows by the river. We can't get back to the Slenderwood in time to find it and get back here before . . ."

*Before Plum dies.* The words hung in the air around them. Leaf let out another moan of grief and licked Plum's ear softly.

"You don't need to return to the Slenderwood," said Shadowhunter.

Leaf looked up. "What?"

The tiger got up and sniffed the air. "The Slenderwood is not the closest part of the river. We've traveled far from there, but the river bends and flows. I have walked these mountains for some time, searching for you. The closest bank is . . ." He turned on the rock, looking back the way they had come, and down the hill to their left and right. Finally his ears swiveled, and he pointed down a steep, almost cliff-edge slope in the direction of the sunrise. "That way. Run, Dragon Speaker, run, and follow the downward path through the valleys, and you shall reach the water before the sun sets."

Leaf was already up on her paws. "Thank you, Shadowhunter. Will you stay with her? Will you make sure the monster doesn't come back?"

"I will." Shadowhunter walked down the side of the rock and sat by Plum's side, curling his tail over her. He licked her wound with his huge, rough tongue, and Plum gasped as she finally saw him, terror and confusion in her eyes.

"What . . . are you . . . ?" she groaned.

"A servant of the Dragon," replied Shadowhunter. "Be still."

"I'll be back soon, Plum," Leaf gabbled. "I'll be back and we'll make you better, I promise."

"The Dragon is with us," Plum sighed, and shut her eyes.

Leaf turned and ran, with Dasher at her heels.

The first descent was the most terrifying. Snow and rock slid under Leaf's paws, and more than once she found herself tumbling, rolling to a stop, getting up and running again. Terror gripped her and she almost couldn't force herself to go on, but then she thought of Plum. If they didn't make it back in time, Plum would die, and Leaf hadn't told her any of the things she wanted to—that she loved her, that she had two siblings, that the Dragon had shown her the way. She hadn't even told her goodbye.

That thought got her up again, every time she fell. It gave her the strength to ignore the bruises, the ache in her lungs, and the cuts on the pads of her paws.

The slope eventually became easier, and the ground warmer and more earth than rock. They ran down between cliffs and along valley floors, sometimes having to pick their way past trees and rocks that had been shaken loose from the higher slopes when the earth growled. They splashed through freezing-cold snowmelt as it streamed down to join the river, and made their way around and past huge columns of rock that seemed to be the last remaining evidence of some much older mountain peak that had once stood there.

High Sun passed, and Leaf gasped the blessing under her breath and kept on running. By Long Light she was starving and weak. She tried to stumble on, but Dasher stood in front of her, and she no longer had the energy even to step around her small friend. She sank to her belly on the ground. Dasher ran off and found a bamboo stalk, dragging it back to her in his teeth. She spoke the blessing aloud, thanking the Dragon for his gift of endurance, and almost collapsed into howls of grief as she spoke the words. But then they ate, and after they had, she got back to her stinging paws. Soon after that they turned a corner and found themselves looking down the valley toward a lush, wooded slope and, beyond the wavering branches, a glimpse of glittering water.

The sight of it put strength back into Leaf's heart.

The journey between the trees was slower, exhaustion creeping back into Leaf's limbs as she had to pick her way between the trunks and over rocks and down slippery, moss-covered slopes. But at last, at Sun Fall, Leaf and Dasher burst out onto a wide, stony bank that sloped gently down to the edge of the water.

Leaf stumbled to an unsteady halt, kicking up pebbles. She looked around for purple leaf, and with a relief so intense it made her dizzy, she saw a stand of distinctive purple bamboo growing out from between two rocks.

But she saw something else, too. At the edge of the water, sodden and still, there was a black-and-white-furred shape.

She ran toward it.

It was a panda cub, half-grown, about Leaf's own age. The panda was lying on her back in the water, paws splayed, her chest rising and falling shallowly. She was still alive, but sleeping, while the river lapped over her back legs and almost up to her chin.

"Got to pull her away from the river," Leaf said, and bent down to try to grab the scruff of her neck so she could drag her back. But as she did, she saw something on the panda's paw.

Her pads were black, except for one. Her grip pad was as white as the snow on the mountain. As white as Leaf's was.

"No," Leaf said. "It can't be . . ."

*But it is.*

*Shadowhunter sent us here. Shadowhunter is a servant of the Dragon.*

*The Great Dragon brought me to this spot, just in time. . . .*

There was no other explanation, and certainly no time to seek one. Leaf grabbed the other panda and pulled her back out of the river. As she did, the panda groaned and coughed. After a few paw steps, she wriggled out of Leaf's grip and flopped over onto her belly.

"Hey! Lemme go . . ."

Leaf backed away, as the panda spat water onto the ground. She staggered upright, taking two attempts but finally standing on four shaking paws. Her fur was matted and sopping wet, and she looked up at Leaf and Dasher with confused anger in her eyes.

"What's . . . who are you? Where am I—is this the Prosperhill? I don't know you. Where's Sunset? I need to . . . he's . . ." She trailed off, catching her breath. Then she blinked, and shook her head, and when she looked back at Leaf, her eyes seemed clearer. "Oh. I remember." She sat back on her haunches. "Where am I? Who are you?"

"You—you aren't going to believe this," Leaf said. Despite the panda's annoyed demeanor, and Plum's desperate situation, and her own bruised and aching body, Leaf's heart was filling up with a kind of joy she had never felt before. She looked into the eyes of the other panda, and then she sprang forward and nuzzled her cheek. "My name is Leaf. I'm your sister!"

# CHAPTER TWENTY-ONE

GHOST JUMPED AS A golden bird took flight from a branch above his head with a loud cry. The leaves above rustled as the bird passed through them and vanished from sight. Ghost stared after it, but there were too many branches and too many leaves—almost as soon as it had moved, it was just *gone*.

There had been birds on the mountain, and plenty of other creatures too, but they had all seemed to stay far away from the leopards and from each other. Down here in this strange green-and-gold land, there seemed to be animals everywhere he looked—beetles, birds, small rodents. He'd even glimpsed a monkey, on a distant hill, swinging from the branch of a tree.

In the forest beyond the mountain, it was warm, and it was damp. Moss grew across the rocks, not even seeming to need earth to root itself in. The ground was soft, and parts of it were wet and stuck to his paws, getting into his fur. Instead of slick ice that could cause a fall, here there was deep mud that seemed to want to suck him in and keep him forever. The hills were just as steep, though not so high, and there were *so many trees*. Even looking down from the high places, half the time he couldn't see the horizon for all the leaves.

It wasn't *bad*, exactly, but he wasn't sure he liked it. He felt crammed into a space that wasn't big enough for him.

"I miss the snow," Shiver said. She shook herself, and cleaned her muzzle with one large paw. "It's *sticky* here."

"We'll get used to it," Ghost said. "There's more prey here, anyway. There must be. We just have to figure out how to hunt it."

*And anyway,* he thought, *we can't go back.*

"I wonder what Snowstorm and Frost are doing," Shiver said softly.

Ghost had been trying not to wonder that. Whatever he pictured his siblings doing, whether they were still mourning Winter or had moved on with their lives, it made him sad to think about it. "Probably hunting," he said stiffly. "And we should do the same. I don't really want to eat bugs *again*, even if they were easy to catch."

"Me neither!" Shiver agreed. "Maybe we should split up. Double our chances."

Ghost felt his heart sink, but then he shook himself. There was no use being sad about it—he was no leopard, and Shiver would do better by herself, even if she had to stop to catch her breath all the time.

"Good idea," he said. Then he added, almost to himself,

"Perhaps I'll figure out how a bear is supposed to hunt."

"Right!" Shiver said brightly, and licked his cheek. "I'll go this way, you go that way, and I'll meet you back here to share what we catch. It'll be fine. Just don't get lost!"

Ghost nodded. He looked around, as Shiver slipped away into the bushes, and tried to study where they were. But everything looked the same to him—trees and rocks, and then more trees. He guessed he would have to make sure to follow his own scent back, or find Shiver's. He could still do that, even if there were a lot of unfamiliar sounds and scents in this strange place.

He started walking, moving slowly and sniffing the air as he went. Unlike the bare slopes of the White Spine, he soon found a prey-scent—and then another, and another, and one that might have been the same one but might just have been very similar. They crisscrossed over the forest floor in such a confusing mess that he sat back on his haunches and scratched at his nose for a moment.

He tried to remember all that Winter had said about hunting. It stung to think of her face, but he had to find something to eat. He recalled that she had once said that if there were prey-scents, but no prey, that meant they would come back. All a leopard had to do was conceal themselves somehow, and wait.

Ghost brightened. That had been hard to do on the bare mountainside, but in this crowded forest there were plenty of places to hide. He crawled under a nearby clump of ferns and settled in to wait.

But the longer he sat there, the more restless he felt. The fur on his belly was getting muddy, and beetles crawled over his paws, and then up and over his back. A fly buzzed around his nose, and he tried to huff it away, and then he tried to ignore it, but the longer he lay there, the louder the buzzing seemed to get, until he lost his temper altogether.

"Get off!" he roared, rearing up and swatting at the fly. It flew away, and so did a bird that had landed in a nearby tree, but now took off with a loud squawk.

Ghost sat up in the ferns and sighed. There was certainly no point staying here now that he'd alerted every prey creature anywhere nearby. He clumsily climbed out of the bush and walked away, shaking his head. If this was how bears were supposed to hunt, he wasn't a much better bear than he had been a leopard.

As he was walking, he heard a strange sound. It sounded like the splashing that the snow made in the summer when it melted and ran down between the rocks. But he could see no water nearby. Puzzled, and happy to have something to distract him from his search for prey, he decided to follow the sound.

It grew louder as he walked downhill, over the mossy rocks. The ground became even wetter, and then he came around a huge tree trunk and saw something in front of him that stopped him in his tracks. Between the trees ahead, there was a stream, just like the ones that formed in the mountain. But it was *enormous*.

Ghost made his way to the edge of the water, treading

carefully, not wanting to fall into this monster of a stream. There was another forest on the other side, with more rocks and trees. But the stream seemed to stretch out forever to his left and right, the impossibly large mass of water rushing along. How much water could there be? How far did it go? If he walked along it, would it finally vanish between the rocks like the streams did, or would it just go on and on?

He carefully dipped a paw into the water. It wasn't as cold as the snowmelt, but it felt good. He suddenly felt thirstier than he ever had before, and he carefully put his face down to the surface and drank. It tasted clear and wonderful. He drank and drank, letting the water splash his face until his fur was wet and his belly was almost full.

"You are thirsty," called a distant voice. "Have you walked a long way, to be so thirsty?"

Ghost's head snapped up, sending a shower of droplets through the air. He turned, looking along the bank of the stream to see who had spoken, but there seemed to be nobody there.

"Over here, friend!" the voice said, and Ghost realized it was coming from the other side of the monstrous stream. He peered across, and saw a shape sitting on a rock that jutted out into the water. It was large and rounded, but he recognized it at once.

It was another bear.

For a moment he couldn't speak, as excitement, fear, and guilt fought each other in his mind. It was the same kind of bear as the one he'd encountered in the cave. In the daylight, he got a clearer look at the markings and saw that there were large circles around the eyes and a stripe over the back and the front legs.

*Does he know that bear from the cave? Will he know I hurt it?*

But then, he had walked all day, and come so far since the cave, and anyway, how would this bear have crossed the massive expanse of water?

His excitement began to push through his fear.

"My name is Ghost," he called back.

"By the Dragon," said the other bear, scratching behind his ear. "I believe you are a panda! A lean and powerful panda, to be certain, and all white."

"What—what's a panda?" Ghost asked.

"Why, we both are!" said the panda.

Ghost stared at him, and then looked down at himself. He didn't have the black markings, and he was more muscular where the other bear was round. But the longer he looked, the more he saw the similarities. Their ears were the same shape, their muzzles the same length.

"I'm a panda," he whispered. Then he said it again, louder, until he roared it across the water to the bear on the other side, splashing his paws in the stream. "A panda! I'm a panda!"

"Didn't you know? Was that why you seemed so unhappy when you first came down the hill?"

Ghost's joy faded a little, and he sat back heavily on his haunches. He felt overwhelmed by all this: the water, the trees, and now this panda—this *other* panda—who spoke to him so kindly. As if he was worth speaking to.

"I did come from far away," Ghost said. "I—I lost my mother. I had to leave my littermates—but they weren't actually my littermates—and my mother, she's dead, and they were right, I didn't belong there, I'm not a leopard, and . . ." He stopped, embarrassed at how little sense this must be making to the kindly panda on the opposite bank. "I came a long way," he said again.

"That sounds very hard," said the panda. "But I'm so glad we've found each other! The Great Dragon must have brought you here. And you may have lost your home, but you've just made a new friend. Ghost the panda, my name is Sunset Deepwood."

# EPILOGUE

Sᴜɴꜱᴇᴛ Dᴇᴇᴘᴡᴏᴏᴅ ɪꜱ ᴀ traitor.

Shadowhunter's tail lashed restlessly, sweeping pine needles from side to side as he paced through the trees, a little way from the clearing where the two panda kittens and the fox-bear were gathered around the one called Plum.

*Sunset Deepwood is alive, but he's turned bad.*

This didn't make any sense.

He didn't doubt the word of the second triplet. The Dragon had clearly sent her to them, across the impassable river, to rejoin her sister and deliver this news. But there was so much about all of this, everything since the flood, that still didn't make sense.

*Where is the third triplet? And why has the prophecy taken so long to come true?*

He wanted to roar his frustration aloud, to snarl up at the

Dragon Mountain for answers, but he restrained himself. It would only frighten the pandas, and they were going to need to trust him.

He returned to the clearing, where Plum was weakly sitting up while Leaf helped her eat the purple leaf. Rain was sitting nearby.

"I'm glad to help," she said. "But listen, my mother's name is *Peony*. It's not Orchid. She's alive, on the other side of the river. None of this makes any sense. You see that, right? Why would having the same colored paw pads mean we're sisters?"

"Have you ever met another panda with the same pad?" Leaf challenged her. "Because I haven't!"

"Well . . . I mean . . . no," Rain admitted. "I haven't. But it still doesn't mean I'm going to believe I'm a *Dragon Speaker*. . . ."

"You will be a Dragon Speaker," Shadowhunter said. Rain looked up and saw him, and he saw the fear and determination in her eyes even as she pulled herself up and turned to face him, as if she believed she could fight a tiger if she had to. "Whether you believe it or not."

Shadowhunter saw a sudden flash of recognition and fear in the eyes of Plum, now that she was coming out of her fever, and dipped his head in acknowledgment. At his paws, he heard a small growl. He looked down into the face of Dasher, and felt his whiskers curl a little in an involuntary smile. The fox-bear was so tiny, yet here he was, growling at a creature he knew could and would devour him if they had met under other circumstances.

*It is good that they have such a brave and faithful friend,* he thought, *however small. They will all need to be brave, before this is over.*

It was difficult to leave them alone on the mountainside, but he knew he had no choice.

"Speaker Leaf, I must depart," he said.

Leaf looked up. "Where are you going? To find our other triplet?"

"Yes—among other things. If you are in danger, make for Fang Top. And may the Great Dragon watch over you all."

He turned to go, and heard Dasher and Rain both let out soft sighs of relief.

"Shadowhunter," Leaf called. He looked back. "May the Great Dragon watch over you, too."

Shadowhunter nodded once, satisfaction in his heart as he bounded lightly over the rocks and between the twisted trees. *She's learning.*

There was a reason the Great Dragon had chosen the tigers, the fiercest creatures in all the Bamboo Kingdom, to act as its Watchers. A tiger watched over every Dragon Speaker, made sure they lived to adulthood, and guided them finally to the lair of the Dragon, where they would come into their full powers. The succession had always gone quickly and smoothly, for countless generations . . . until now.

*The Great Dragon must have a great deal of faith in me*, he thought wryly, *to give me three Dragon Speakers to bring to its lair all at once, and to scatter them across the kingdom.*

*Or is it four . . . ?*

What could have happened to Sunset Deepwood, to turn him into a liar who would attempt to drown his own successor?

It felt like much more than a year since the night before the flood, when he and Sunset had met by the river. Sunset had been unable to stop pacing the bank, worry streaming from him in waves that made the tiger's muzzle curl. He had told Shadowhunter that he was about to die. Shadowhunter hadn't wanted to believe it, but Sunset had been too preoccupied with what would come afterward to accept his sympathies or his grief. He had told the tiger all about the prophecy, about the triplets who would come after him. He had all but begged Shadowhunter to protect them.

"No matter what happens, my old friend," he had said, "promise me you will guard them with your life."

Sunset, it seemed, now had other plans. But Shadowhunter had made that promise, and he intended to keep it.

*No Watcher has ever failed their Speaker, and I will not be the first.*

He would get to the root of Sunset's behavior, and he would deliver the triplets to the Dragon to face their destiny.

But first he needed to hunt. He turned his muzzle to the sky, the stars glinting above him, and scented the air. Then he sprang from his perch and bounded away, toward the heart of the Bamboo Kingdom.